SPOILING FOR A FIGHT

The big blond cowpuncher's muscles were like solid rock, and his grip on the butt of Fargo's pistol was impossible to pry loose. Fargo was aware of the two other men nearby, and he kept rolling with the big man so they couldn't get a clear shot at him. They rolled up against the big rock, with the blond man on top, and Fargo saw his chance. Summoning all his strength, he jerked the man's heavy arm hard against the rock, smashing the fist holding his Colt with a bone-shattering jolt.

The blond man yowled in pain and his grip loosened. Fargo wrenched his pistol free. He jammed his left into the man's gut and heard the breath leave him. In the next instant Fargo smashed the man's head against the rock as well, and he fell heavily forward onto Fargo.

Fargo didn't have time to enjoy his triumph. He had two more hard cases to take care of. But that was fine with him. He had been sparring with spirits for too long. It was a pleasure to be up against flesh and blood. . . .

THE TRAILSMAN #157
GHOST RANCH MASSACRE

THE TRAILSMAN

157

GHOST RANCH
MASSACRE

by

Jon Sharpe

A SIGNET BOOK

SIGNET
Published by the Penguin Group
Penguin Books USA Inc.. 375 Hudson Street.
New York. New York 10014. U.S.A.
Penguin Books Ltd. 27 Wrights Lane.
London W8 5TZ. England
Penguin Books Australia Ltd. Ringwood.
Victoria. Australia
Penguin Books Canada Ltd. 10 Alcorn Avenue.
Toronto. Ontario. Canada M4V 3B2
Penguin Books (N.Z.) Ltd. 182–190 Wairau Road.
Auckland 10. New Zealand

Penguin Books Ltd. Registered Offices:
Harmondsworth. Middlesex. England

First published by Signet. an imprint of Dutton Signet.
a division of Penguin Books USA Inc.

First Printing. January. 1995
10 9 8 7 6 5 4 3 2 1

The first chapter of this book originally appeared in *The Sawdust Trail*.
the one hundred fifty-sixth volume of this series.

 REGISTERED TRADEMARK—MARCA REGISTRADA

Printed in the United States of America

The Trailsman

Beginnings . . . they bend the tree and they mark the man. Skye Fargo was born when he was eighteen. Terror was his midwife, vengeance his first cry. Killing spawned Skye Fargo, ruthless, cold-blooded murder. Out of the acrid smoke of gunpowder still hanging in the air, he rose, cried out a promise never forgotten.

The Trailsman they began to call him all across the West: searcher, scout, hunter, the man who could see where others only looked, his skills for hire but not his soul, the man who lived each day to the fullest, yet trailed each tomorrow. Skye Fargo, the Trailsman, and the seeker who could take the wildness of a land and the wanting of a woman and make them his own.

*1860, in the vastness of the mysterious Hopi lands
that will one day be called Arizona . . .
where magic is real
and an ancient spirit returns for revenge*

1

"No! No! Please don't!" she screamed, her dark eyes wide with terror. Above her stood the black-caped man, a long, glittering sword in his hand. He plunged it downward and she shrieked.

"Don't! Don't! It's really hurting me!"

He took up another and drove it in horizontally while she screamed again, a jewel-studded slipper slipping off her foot as she jerked in agony.

"Please! Please stop!"

Skye Fargo watched as the man drove a third blade through the coffin-shaped box and into the body of the ebony-haired woman locked inside, only her head and feet protruding. She moaned. The sound died in her throat and her head fell to one side.

"Oh, it is terrible, is it not?" the magician said in a liquid, accented voice as he advanced toward the foot-lights. He swirled the cape about him, and his huge, protruding black eyes seemed to look into the face of each member of the audience. "To see the beautiful Arabella die such a horrible death! What a frightful loss! But I, Magnus the Magnificent, I have learned the secrets of life and death, the ancient mysteries from the line of Zoroaster . . ."

Fargo smiled to himself. It was a damned good

trick. It really looked like the long swords had gone right through the woman's body. As the magician prattled on, Fargo's eyes swept the stage and he saw, beneath the box, the slow dripping of red blood. A pool was gathering on the floor below. Several others noticed it too.

"She's really dead!" a woman cried out.

"The blood! She's bleeding!" a man in the first row shouted at the magician. The man, wearing overalls and a straw hat, stood up and pointed anxiously.

Magnus the Magnificent refused to look and only waved the man down, as if not believing him, and continued to talk hocus-pocus. The audience grew restless with tension. Several more men jumped to their feet and shouted at the magician. But Magnus ignored them and continued to try to speak over the babble. A woman in a bonnet sitting near Fargo sobbed into her handkerchief.

Fargo began to wonder if something really had gone wrong with the trick. He stared at the box on stage and at the dark-haired beauty named Arabella. Her lovely face was turned toward the audience, eyes closed, long black hair flowing down to the ground. Fargo kept his gaze on her and then saw the barest twitch of an eyelid and the flare of her nostrils as she took a breath. She was alive, he thought, relieved. So, the dripping red liquid was just another part of the trick. He smiled to himself. It was a damned good show.

The audience was in a near riot now, most of them standing and stamping their feet, trying to get the magician to turn around and look. The pooled fake blood beneath the box began to run in a rivulet down the raked stage toward the footlights. Just then, Magnus paused in his speech and glanced down. He did a double take as he saw the trickling red blood, and his face took on an expression of horror.

"Oh, my God!" he shrieked. Magnus whirled about and advanced upstage to look at the blood under the box. He paced, wrung his hands, and tore at his mass of wild gray hair, as if in helpless despair. The audience went wild. Women cried and men were on their feet, shouting for a doctor and waving their hats in the air. Suddenly, Magnus snapped back toward the audience and held up his hands with a grand gesture. The theater fell silent.

"What a tragedy," Magnus said, a sob catching his sonorous voice. "Such a terrible thing has never happened to me before."

Yeah, not since the last show, Fargo thought wryly to himself. The magician laid his hand on the wooden box and bowed his head. Several women sniffled.

"Murderer! Arrest him!" a man shouted.

"Wait!" Magnus said, raising his large head. "There is but one hope! One small possibility . . ." The audience was hanging on his every word. Magnus drew a small glass vial from his cape and held it up. "The elixir of life—three drops of this precious fluid were given to me by Zarcon of Arabia. I hope to God it will be enough."

Magnus intoned some magic words, waved the tiny bottle over the wooden box, then unstoppered it and poured the contents over the top. A loud explosion, followed by a puff of red smoke, made everyone in the small theater jump. When the smoke had cleared, Magnus began pulling the swords slowly out of the box as the audience held its breath. Then Magnus snapped his fingers in front of the woman's face and she opened her eyes and smiled.

"Where am I?" Arabella said, as if confused. "I was having a dream about some angels . . ."

The audience broke out into frenzied applause and relieved laughter as Magnus unlocked the box and helped her out. Arabella jumped down, retrieved her slipper, and took a bow. Fargo admired again her tiny hourglass figure in the tight red sequined costume and the way the color set off the smooth skin of her deep cleavage and waving ebony hair. He wondered if she was busy after the show.

Magnus and Arabella disappeared behind the red curtain, and Frederico the Fantastical Conjurer, a red-mustached man in a blue silk turban, appeared and performed some card tricks, pulled chickens out of empty barrels, and made bouquets of flowers appear out of nowhere. All the while, Frederico kept up a humorless banter that was about as appealing as a sopping wet bedroll. To pass the time, Fargo looked about at the audience, noting the spiffed-up citizens of Cedar City sitting alongside the fresh-scrubbed ranchers' wives in their homespun. When Frederico finished, they applauded politely but unenthusiastically. Then Magnus returned, wearing a yellow brocade vest and a red satin cape, leading Arabella, who had changed into a flowing green gown, low cut and covered with silver stars and planets. The gaslights dimmed as Magnus helped Arabella onto a tall carved throne that had been brought onstage. With a flourish, Magnus blindfolded her and plugged her ears with cotton.

"Please notice that she cannot see or hear anything," Magnus said as he strode to center stage. "And now, esteemed ladies and gentlemen—the grand finale! I would not want to leave you with the terrible memory of the tragedy that almost happened this afternoon." Magnus paused and shuddered visibly. "No, my friends, now we will perform for you the most extraordinary feat of human endeavors . . . the reading of the human mind! Yes! The beautiful Arabella was born with the remarkable gift of mind reading. And now, all I need is a volunteer from the audience."

Magnus stepped up to the footlights and peered out toward the audience. He searched the faces slowly and then locked eyes with Fargo.

"You, sir. No, you there, with the beard. Please come onstage."

Fargo got to his feet with a grin. This should be fun. The secret of this trick was probably a simple one, he thought. Magnus would ask him questions and Arabella could probably hear the answers because the cotton stuck in her ears was fake. Well, he'd just give false answers, he decided. And then see what would happen. Fargo hopped onto the stage. Magnus shook his hand, his protuberant black eyes gleaming. The magician opened his mouth to speak, but Arabella's voice interrupted. Her voice was odd and seemed to come from all around them and at the same moment from very far away.

"There is no need to ask him questions," Arabella cut in. "I can read this man's mind very easily. He is an open book. Since I cannot hear you, touch my hand when you want me to begin."

"She already knows it is a man, even though she is blindfolded," Magnus pointed out to the audience. He turned to Fargo. "We have never met before, have we?" Magnus asked pointedly.

"Never," Fargo said.

"Fine. When Arabella speaks, you will shake your head 'yes' if she speaks the truth and 'no' if she is wrong." Magnus advanced to the throne and touched Arabella's arm.

"This man is a wanderer," Arabella began.

Fargo nodded. Most men were, he thought. In one way or another.

"He rides alone."

That too could be said of a lot of men, he thought as he nodded again.

"He is looking for a job now."

Fargo smiled. She was good.

"And a woman. He is always looking for a woman. Preferably several women."

Fargo laughed, as did most of the audience. A few well-dressed matrons got up and left in a huff.

"He rides a black-and-white horse and he is very famous."

"Is that true?" Magnus asked Fargo, his voice edged with amazement.

"Yeah, I guess," Fargo said with a modest shrug, wondering how she had found out who he was. Arabella paused and raised her head, as if listening to the voices of the mysterious beyond.

"His name . . . is Skye Fargo," she said. The audience murmured as some people recognized his name. "And in his right jacket pocket you will find a purple handkerchief."

"She got the name right, but there's no—" Fargo reached into his pocket to turn it inside out and felt something inside. He pulled out a purple handkerchief. Fargo laughed with astonishment and wondered when they had slipped it into his pocket.

As the audience applauded, Arabella removed her blindfold and came forward, grasping Fargo's hand and pulling him toward the footlights. She and Magnus took a bow. The audience cheered. Fargo squeezed her hand and she glanced toward him.

"What are you doing after the show?" Fargo asked her above the noise. "Can I take you to dinner?"

"That would be lovely," she said with a smile, her dark eyes dancing with light. "Come to the stage door."

Fargo jumped down off the stage. Magnus the Magnificent and Arabella took several more bows and then the curtain rang down. The buzzing audience got up to leave.

Outside, the clapboard buildings of Cedar City baked in the July afternoon sun. Fargo rounded the brick theater and found the stage door in the alley. A burly man in a tweed cap positioned himself astride the open door. Inside, Fargo could see piles of crates and feathered costumes in heaps.

"Miss Arabella asked me to come see her," Fargo explained. The burly man eyed him suspiciously.

"Oh, yeah? I've heard that story before."

Just then, Arabella hurried by, dressed in the red sequined costume.

"Oh, miss," the burly man called out. "This fella says you asked him to come see you."

Arabella stopped and stared at Fargo. The color rose in her cheeks and her dark eyes flashed.

"I certainly did not," she said. She moved away.

Fargo swore inwardly. Okay, if she didn't want to go to dinner, she could have just said so. The burly man smirked.

"Move off, buddy."

Fargo turned to go. The sound of angry voices drew his attention. They came from the other side of a brightly painted wagon standing at the far end of the alley. On the tall wooden sides of the wagon, in the midst of gold stars and comets, was written: MAGNUS THE MAGNIFICENT, THE WORLD'S GREATEST MAGICIAN. Underneath, in smaller letters, had been added: WITH FREDERICO, THE FANTASTICAL CONJURER. Fargo went to see what was going on. He rounded the wagon and then ducked back behind the corner, remaining just out of sight.

"You low-down cheating bastard!"

A bald, mustached man had spoken. He stood holding a metal box firmly under one arm while Magnus was desperately trying to wrench it from him.

"I'm not cheating you!" Magnus said. "We agreed you'd get twenty-five percent."

"Well, it ain't enough now," the bald man replied, snatching the box out of the magician's grasp. "You're just trying to keep me down because you don't want us getting married."

"I pay you more than you deserve. Give me that money!" Magnus shouted, his face reddening with fury.

The bald man drew a short pistol and aimed it at the older man.

"You're crazy," Magnus said slowly, staring down the barrel of the bald man's pistol.

"You never listen to me, Magnus. You don't take me seriously," the man said. "I've been with this two-bit road show for a year now, and, I tell you, I want more than twenty-five percent."

"No," Magnus said. "Absolutely not. And what are you going to do? Shoot me?"

"Sure," the bald man said. "Some men came up the alley and tried to take your cash. Somebody shot you and I drove them off."

This had gone far enough, Fargo decided. He stepped out from behind the wagon, Colt in hand.

"Drop it," Fargo said.

The bald man whirled at the sound of his voice and instinctively pulled the trigger. The bullet sped through empty space as Fargo leaped to one side and then straight at the man while holstering his Colt. Fargo hit him full force, knocking him into the dust. The cash box went flying. Fargo chopped at the man's hand and he dropped his pistol as they rolled over and over, grappling. The bald man was surprisingly strong, with wiry muscles. He drove his fist into Fargo's jaw, and the alley spun for a second. Fargo pulled back, shaking his head to clear it. Just then, the bald man aimed another blow at Fargo's face, but Fargo brought up his left arm fast. The clout was deflected as Fargo brought his right back in and then sank a hard punch into the man's gut. The breath left him and he lay gasping like a fish on the ground, his green eyes furious. Fargo got to his feet and stood over the bald man.

"You want more?" Fargo asked, covering the man with the Colt.

A furious look was his only answer.

"Should I let him up?" Fargo asked, directing the question at Magnus, who had retrieved the metal cash box. The magician nodded slowly, his eyes on the bald man, who got to his feet with exasperated, jerky motions.

"You're *nothing*, Frederico," Magnus spat. Fargo looked again at the bald man and only then recog-

17

nized him as the untalented conjurer in the show. The bald Frederico looked a lot different without his silk turban. "*Nothing*! Got it? You're a lousy performer," Magnus continued, spitting the words, his large eyes dark with anger. "No talent at all. I've tried to help you, teach you something about magic. And this is the thanks I get! You try to steal from me!"

"You . . . you just don't want me to marry your daughter," Frederico shot back.

So, Arabella was probably the magician's daughter, Fargo thought. And if she was engaged to Frederico, that explained why she wouldn't have dinner with him. But then why did she say yes in the first place?

"Shut up!" Magnus snapped. "And get out. Get your gear out of this wagon. I don't want to see your face again. Ever."

Frederico beat the dust out of his clothes and stomped toward the rear of the enclosed painted wagon. He jerked open the back door. Fargo glanced inside curiously. The wagon was half-filled with stacks of colorful scenery, large mirrors, and other equipment that Fargo couldn't identify. Frederico pulled several bags out of the back while Magnus watched.

"That one's mine," Magnus cut in. Frederico angrily slung a canvas bag back into the wagon and slammed the doors. Magnus stepped forward and padlocked them shut.

"Now, get out," he said to Frederico.

The bald man stalked down the alley while Magnus watched him go. Just then, Arabella appeared at the stage door, dressed in the green gown with silver planets. She glanced at the retreating Frederico with a worried look.

"Did you quarrel with him, Father?" she asked Magnus.

"I told him to get out," Magnus said. "And it's about time."

Arabella nodded thoughtfully. "So much for the wedding," she said softly, but without any emotion. Fargo wondered at her complete lack of feelings. Why had Arabella planned to marry Frederico if she hadn't even cared for him? Her gaze shifted and she seemed to notice him for the first time.

"Mr. Fargo!" she said. "I thought maybe you'd forgotten. Are you still interested in dinner?"

Fargo felt completely confused. She was as changeable as a cloud on a breezy day.

"Sure," he said doubtfully.

"I'll change my clothes. Be back in just a moment," Arabella said.

"Ahem," the magician said, as he inspected Fargo. "So, you are taking my daughter to dinner."

"That's right," Fargo said with a smile. "Any objections?"

The magician's face wrinkled in a smile. "I've heard your reputation. You're the one they call the Trailsman. Honest man." Magnus's face darkened. "But likes women."

"Well," Fargo said, "I'm honest with women, too."

Magnus smiled slowly. "Arabella is a grown woman. She will be fine with you," he said with a twinkle.

Just then she reappeared at the stage door, wearing the red sequined suit again. Fargo wondered if she meant to wear it to dinner.

"What have you done?" she shouted, running toward Magnus. She reached out as if to scratch her father as he caught her arms. She collapsed, sobbing, against the old man.

"He wasn't worthy of you," Magnus said, patting her shoulder. "Forget him. Forget him. There'll be other men. Much better men."

Fargo was just beginning to wonder if Arabella was stark raving mad when he heard her voice behind him.

"I'm ready!"

She stood at the stage door, decked out in a red-and-white-striped dress with a matching parasol. The dress was cut low to show the curves of her breasts. Fargo stared at Arabella and back at the sobbing woman in Magnus's arms. The two women—twins, obviously—were as alike as two pins in a pincushion.

"That's right," Arabella said, seeing the amazement on Fargo's face. She hooked her arm through his. "This is Adrienne, my twin sister."

Adrienne, hearing her name, looked up and wiped the tears away with the back of her hand. Magnus put his arm around her.

"My two girls," the magician said proudly. "They are wonderful onstage. And they come in very handy in many of our tricks."

Fargo remembered one of the tricks he had seen in the show, in which Arabella had been locked into a box onstage and made to disappear in a puff of smoke. Just an instant later—too fast for her to have gone through a trapdoor and run under the theater beneath the audience—she had appeared at the back of the house. Now Fargo laughed as he realized how it had been done.

"Let's go," he said, touching his hat brim to Adrienne as he escorted Arabella down the alleyway and into the street.

"Get her home before midnight!" Magnus called after them.

"Not likely," Arabella whispered to Fargo.

As they swept up the boardwalk, Arabella's red-and-white dress and her curvaceous figure drew some appreciative glances from the other men. She didn't seem to notice, but bent her attention entirely on Fargo as he told her about his work and his adventures on the trails of the West.

An hour later they were seated in the dining room of the Cedar City Hotel. Fargo had just ordered roast beef, potatoes, and fresh asparagus and was refilling Arabella's glass with red burgundy when the waiter walked up.

"A telegram for you, sir," he said, handing a folded paper to Fargo.

Fargo felt a rush of mild surprise. The only person who knew he was in Cedar City was old Colonel Parkin, a retired officer who lived off to the north of town and whom Fargo had known years before in Kansas Territory. Fargo had visited the colonel several days before on his way into town to find another trail-blazing job. He opened the paper and glanced first at the name of the sender. The telegram was from Hank Giffin. Memory stirred in Fargo. He remembered Giffin. Sergeant Giffin, one of Parkin's best men.

"Trouble?" Arabella asked.

Fargo nodded absentmindedly and read the telegram.

FOUND YOUR WHEREABOUTS TODAY FROM THE COLONEL. NEED HELP. BAD TROUBLE HERE IN MIRAGE. LIFE OR DEATH. COME IF YOU CAN. HANK GIFFIN.

"Yeah, it's trouble," Fargo said, tucking the telegram into his shirt. He called the waiter over and flipped him a gold eagle, asking him to send off a telegram to Mirage saying he'd be there in three days' time. After the waiter bustled off, Fargo sat back for a moment, his thoughts far away. He'd been through the town of Mirage once, a tiny settlement at the edge of the Hopi lands a hundred miles southeast of Cedar City. Strange country around there—colorful empty desert with weird rock formations. Fargo shook off the memory as the dinner arrived.

All during the meal, Fargo successfully pushed away thoughts of Hank Giffin and the trouble in Mirage. Arabella was good company, he discovered. She had a ready laugh and a quick wit. They were waiting for the dessert and coffee to arrive when he remembered to ask her something that had been bothering him.

"So, how did you read my mind?" he asked with a wink.

Arabella dimpled. She picked up her dinner napkin and placed it on her head, holding it under her chin like a scarf.

"Excuse me, sir," she said in a cracked voice. Fargo started, then laughed, remembering the old blind woman in smoked glasses who had been begging in front of the Cedar City Theater before the magic show started. After he had dropped a half-dollar in her tin cup, she stopped him and they had spoken for just a minute. But, he realized, from that brief conversation the disguised Arabella had found out his name. The rest she might have known from his reputation, which had got around.

"How'd you know about my Ovaro?"

"Your horse?" she asked with a giggle. "I saw you tether it to a post before you came up to buy a ticket."

"I guess there's an explanation for every trick," Fargo laughed. "My favorite one was the floating . . ."

"The Wondrous Floating Woman," Arabella interjected, imitating her father's magisterial pronunciation.

"How did you do that one?" Fargo asked, remembering the astonishing sight of Arabella lying down, suspended in thin air six feet above the stage.

"Oh, no," Arabella said, suddenly serious. "That is one of my father's most famous tricks. There are a lot of other magicians who would like to get their hands on it."

"Like Frederico?"

Arabella's face darkened.

"He just wants money," she said. "And my sister. Well, she's desperately in love with him."

"Did he ever bother you?" Fargo asked.

"Not since the first show I saw him do," Arabella said. "I laughed at him when he pulled a rabbit out of his hat and it made a mess down the front of his coat." She giggled at the memory. "He's trouble. I don't know what Adrienne sees in that man. Maybe she just feels sorry for him."

Fargo glanced toward the door of the dining room as he heard a loud voice. A familiar voice.

"Well, speak of the devil," Fargo said, looking over Arabella's shoulder. Frederico staggered in and stood swaying in the doorway. His collar was unbuttoned and his jacket was askew. His eyes were unfocused and he'd obviously been drinking. The bald man stared into the dining room, then spotted Fargo and Arabella. He headed for their table. The other patrons fell silent as they watched him weaving unsteadily through the tables.

"What the hell are you doing, stranger?" Frederico shouted. "You're going out with my girl!" A waiter hurried toward the intruder, but backed away when Frederico drew a knife from inside his jacket. As Frederico approached, Fargo stood slowly, all six feet of him, and Arabella turned around in her chair to look at the drunken man. Fargo noticed Arabella kept her wits about her.

"Get out of here, Frederico," Arabella said, her voice low but commanding. "And do my sister a favor—leave her alone."

"You heard what the lady said," Fargo added, resting his hand lightly on the butt of his pistol.

Frederico, seeing her face, backed away a few steps.

"Oh, it's you," he said, recognizing Arabella. The bald man shot a look of pure hatred at Fargo and sheathed his knife. He blinked a few times and held onto a nearby table for support. Then he turned and staggered out.

The dining room was abuzz, with everyone asking who he was and what was going on. The feathered and fringed ladies of Cedar City craned their necks to stare at Arabella as they gossiped. Fargo heard the words "magic show" and knew she'd been recognized. Arabella seemed suddenly uncomfortable. The waiter appeared.

"Is everything alright here?" he asked. Fargo noticed that Arabella was squirming under the scrutiny and curiosity of the other diners. Somewhere quieter would be nice, he decided.

"Do you have private dining rooms?" Fargo asked the waiter.

"Yes. Several. There is one available right now."

"We'll take coffee there," Fargo said. Arabella shot him a look of gratitude, and he rose to escort her from the room.

The private dining room was hung in red velvet curtains and furnished with a small dining table, two chairs, and a large settee. A grandfather clock stood in one corner and several fine paintings hung on the walls. The oil lamps were turned low. As he held her chair, Arabella sank into it with a sigh of relief.

"This is much better," she said, looking around.

She was as pretty a woman as Fargo had ever seen, he thought as he looked down at her. The dark mass of ringlets fell over her smooth shoulders, and her black eyes shone with intelligence and humor. From this vantage point, he looked down into her bodice and saw the swell of her breasts and the tunnel of cleavage between them. She looked up at him.

Fargo bent over her and kissed her lightly, exploring. Her hand came up behind his head and played with his earlobe. Fargo nibbled at her lips and flicked his tongue delicately as he felt her mouth open; then she was taking his tongue deep into her mouth as if hungry for him.

The door opened and the waiter entered with a silver tray. Fargo straightened up as the waiter, his eyes downcast and pretending not to have seen them, approached the table. He poured coffee, set slices of chocolate cake in front of them, and beat a hasty retreat. As soon as the door shut behind him, Arabella giggled.

"I was waiting all night for you to do that," she said, a smile in her voice.

"Where were we?" Fargo said, bending over her again. This time he kissed her deeply, enjoying the fresh, sweet taste of her. She ran her hands over his strong back and he spanned her slender waist between his big hands. He moved one hand upward, cupping her full breast as she murmured in her throat.

"Oh, Skye," she whispered, "I've been hearing about you for years. And then this afternoon, when I found out your name and . . . I hoped I would meet you. And I hoped . . . I hoped this would happen." Fargo stood and pulled her up out of her chair, holding her close, inhaling the perfume of her hair.

"I'm moving on tomorrow, Arabella," he said. "This telegram—there's trouble out near the Hopi lands. And I've got to go. You understand that?"

"I do," she said. She gazed up at him, her eyes serious. "But at least we have tonight."

Fargo kissed her again and she held nothing back, even grasping his hand and guiding him again toward her swelling breast. This time he slipped his hand inside the plunging neckline of her dress and her breast overfilled his hand. He gently rubbed the warm nipple between two of his fingers and she moaned.

"Oh, yes," she said. "Let's."

Fargo moved away from her toward the door. He was glad to see that there was a brass lock on the door. Not enough to stop someone determined to get inside, but enough to deter a waiter and avoid an embarrassing situation. He threw the bolt and turned back toward her.

Arabella had moved to the settee. Her dress billowed around her, a huge cloud of red-and-white stripes. Fargo crossed the room and knelt on the carpet in front of her. He inched her dress up to her knee and bent to kiss her stockinged leg, flicking his tongue across the silk-clad flesh.

"You wicked man," she said with a laugh. Fargo kissed upward, circling her knee and proceeding up her thigh. She pulled her dress up higher about her, and his mouth reached her scented garters, the tops of her stockings, and then he was kissing the bare flesh of her thighs. The warm, musky odor among the lace made him feel suddenly drunk with desire. He hardened with wanting.

"You're going to love this," he murmured.

2

Fargo inhaled Arabella's sweet odor as he nuzzled the warm, bare flesh above the tops of her silken stockings. Her lace petticoats and skirt billowed about him. He heard her sigh with pleasure as he nosed her soft mound, covered by silk panties.

"Oh, Skye," she whispered. "Yes. Yes. It might be for only one night, but I want you."

Fargo's fingers gently pulled at the panties, and Arabella shifted on the settee until they inched down her legs and she kicked them off. Fargo pulled her petticoats up again and plunged beneath them until he found the folded wetness of her. He flicked his tongue across her soft knot and felt it harden, engorged with desire.

"Oh, God!" she moaned. Arabella's hands clutched at his shoulders as he tasted her. He moved his hand up and found she had loosened her dress so that her breasts now spilled out over the top of her bodice. He sought a tender nipple and found it, massaging it gently as her hips began moving as if she could not help herself. Arabella moaned rhythmically as he drank her in, teasing and caressing.

He felt her lean forward over him, and her hands moved downward across his broad back and fumbled at his belt. She brushed across his Levi's and felt for his long rigidity, straining at the fabric. She undid his belt as Fargo trembled with desire, all the time nuzzling her as she undid his trousers and took him in her soft, cool hands. His hot throbbing grew larger.

"Yes, yes," she said.

Fargo emerged from beneath her skirts and pulled her hips toward him on the settee as she lay back. She gasped as he eased, by slow, delightful degrees, his massiveness into her slick, warm sheath. Then he began to pulse slowly back and forth as he cupped her large breasts in his hands, angling upward against her tight folds and the center of her pleasure.

"Oh, God. Oh, Skye. Yes, yes. I'm almost there," she murmured.

He could feel the welling begin, the gathering of heat. He slowed, brought his hand down to touch again her tiny, hard knot.

"Oh, yes! Yes!" she screamed, bucking under him, contracting around him with waves of ecstasy.

Fargo held nothing back now but thrust into her, letting himself go, pouring his passion into her, shooting again and again, in beating contractions, until he thought it would never end. Finally, he slowed, stopped, fell forward onto her. Arabella held him in her arms.

"Oh, my darling," she breathed into his ear. "Oh, yes."

Fargo felt the blackness of sleep come up around him, and for a few moments, let himself sink into oblivion, even as he knelt on the floor before the settee and she held him cradled on her breast. After a few minutes, Fargo stirred and felt the exhaustion leave him. He turned his head and smiled up at her.

"Now *that* was magic," he said.

After a while, they pulled on their clothes again, reluctantly. The coffee was cold, but they sat down to the chocolate cake. Fargo unlocked the door and summoned the waiter, who appeared with fresh hot coffee and disappeared again discreetly. Arabella, the color high in her cheeks and her mass of wavy dark hair wild around her face and shoulders, had the look of a contented cat.

"So, what was the bad news in that telegram?" she asked.

Fargo pulled it out of his shirt and looked at it again.

"News from an old soldier I knew in Kansas," he answered. "Some kind of trouble down in Mirage. Down near the Hopi lands."

"Mirage. Mirage," Arabella said slowly. "That sounds familiar, somehow." Her brows lowered for a few moments, and then she shook her head, giving up the attempt to remember. "Maybe we did a show there sometime. Is it dangerous down there, with those Indians?"

Fargo laughed.

"Oh, the Hopis are peaceful. Not like Apache. Or the Blackfoot. But they're a strange people," he said.

"Strange? How?"

"Otherworldly," Fargo answered. "A Hopi looks at the world in an unexpected way. The legends go way back, and they have secret rituals no outsider has ever discovered."

"So, they're not dangerous."

"Oh, I wouldn't go that far," Fargo said. "The Hopis will protect what's theirs, all right. I wouldn't step on their toes. But they don't attack without provocation."

He looked again at the telegram.

"I guess the trouble isn't with the Hopis, then," Arabella said.

"Hard to say," Fargo replied. "But I'll have to get on the Piñon Trail first thing in the morning. With luck, I'll be in Mirage in a few days." He glanced at the grandfather clock, which read eleven-thirty. "I can even get you back to your father before you turn into a pumpkin," he added with a smile.

The night wind sweeping across the high Sierra Nevada mountains to the west had turned cold. It whistled around the corners of the buildings in Cedar City. Arabella wrapped her shawl around her and took Fargo's arm as they stepped out the front door of the hotel.

They made their way through the dark, deserted streets toward the boardinghouse next to the theater where Magnus and his daughters were quartered. The large brick playhouse had just come into view when a light glimmered in the alleyway and Fargo heard a mournful wail.

"Wait here," Fargo said to Arabella, pushing her into a doorway and drawing his Colt. He ran forward on silent feet and slid around the corner of the theater to peer into the alley. There, in the middle of the narrow, empty passage, stood Magnus. In one hand he held a lantern. As Fargo watched, the magician raised his head again and made the terrible noise Fargo had heard before—a drawn-out moaning, as if he were in hideous pain.

"Hey! Magnus! What's going on?" Fargo shouted.

31

At the sound of his voice, the old magician turned, hunching down as if to attack. Then he raised the lantern, peered into the gloom, and recognized Fargo.

"Disaster!" Magnus said, his usual booming voice thin and weak. "I am finished. Through." The magician gestured down the empty alley. "It's gone. The most precious thing I own. My life's work."

"The wagon," Fargo said.

"Stolen," Magnus said. "Along with all my magic tricks. And my devices! I designed most of them myself! And I had them made in Europe. I can never, ever replace them. Oh, I am ruined."

"Frederico," Fargo guessed.

"I'm sure of it," Magnus said. "And he could have been gone for hours already. After I dined, I didn't bother to check on the wagon, but went straight to bed. And then, a nightmare awakened me. I hardly knew why, but I got dressed and came outside to look."

Fargo heard light, tentative footsteps behind them.

"It's your father," he called to Arabella. She stepped into the alley. "The wagon's gone. Probably Frederico."

"Oh, no!" she exclaimed. She ran to her father and wrapped her arms around him. "But, Papa! We can't do the show without the things in the wagon. This is terrible!"

"He can't have gone far," Fargo said. "In the morning, we'll tell the sheriff. He'll get a posse together and go after him."

"Oh, no! Oh, no!" Magnus held up a hand in dismay. "We must not call the authorities. Never! Never! It would be better to lose the wagon than to let them hunt him down."

Fargo shot a puzzled look at Arabella, who was worriedly concentrating on her father.

"Why not call the law?" he asked.

"Because," answered Magnus, "if the sheriff catches Frederico, then he and his men will look into the wagon. And that they must never do." Magnus pulled himself upright and his voice took on the stentorian tones that Fargo remembered from the magic show. "Inside that wagon are the secrets of Zoroaster," Magnus said, waving one arm. "Tricks that no other magician has ever even imagined! Mechanical devices I have spent my life perfecting. Mechanisms that can fool the eye and the mind. No, no! If a posse found that wagon and went through it, the art of magic would be lost forever. These professional secrets, which all magicians are sworn not to reveal, would become known to everyone. It would be a catastrophe. No sheriff! I won't hear of it."

"But, Father," Arabella said, "without the equipment, we can't do the show. How will we make a living?" Magnus hung his head. She turned to Fargo. "Please, Skye. Please help us. We'll pay. Anything. Please. Just help." Magnus glanced up, hope in his eyes.

Fargo looked at the pair as he thought of Hank Giffin's desperate telegram. A man's life was in danger down in Mirage. And on the other hand, a wagon full of magic tricks was missing.

"Look," Fargo explained gently, "there's that trouble down in the Hopi lands. I sent my promise I'd go." He paused and saw Arabella sag against her father in despair. "I'll do what I can," he added.

With luck, Frederico, driving the wagon filled with magic tricks, wouldn't have gone far, Fargo thought.

He found out from Magnus where his team of six matched grays was boarded. That was the first place to check. Fargo left Magnus and Arabella and made his way to the Cedar City Livery. The stables were dark and locked up tight. Fargo pounded on the door of the shack at one corner of the fenced yard.

"Whadaya want?" a gruff voice shouted from inside.

"Somebody stole a wagon," Fargo called out. "I need some information."

The door was unbolted. It eased open a crack to reveal a man's suspicious eye and the short barrel of a pistol. "Who are ya?"

Fargo spoke his name and the door opened.

A squat man stood there in his undershirt and trousers. "I remember you," he said. "The black-and-white beauty's yours."

"That's right," Fargo said. "And I need my Ovaro now. Did somebody come by earlier this evening and take that team of matched grays?"

"Sure," the man answered. "The guy who brought 'em here in the first place. One of them theater folks. Mustache. And a bald head. Paid the bill and took 'em."

"About what time?" Fargo asked.

"Right after supper, maybe," he said.

Fargo swore under his breath. So, Frederico had probably skipped town right after his appearance in the hotel dining room. That meant he'd got a good start. Maybe four hours.

"Any idea where he was heading?" Fargo asked.

"Well, now," the stable owner said, scratching his head, "I remember he'd been drinking. Come to think of it, he did ask me a question. Now, what was it?"

After a few moments, he brightened. "Oh, yeah. Asked me how to get to Denver City."

Fargo felt a rush of hope. The trail that led from Cedar City across the Rockies to the mile-high city was a rugged one. It climbed over the saddles of rock-ridged mountains and plunged into deep canyons. The loaded wagon wouldn't make very good time, compared to a pursuing pinto. The stable owner unlocked the barn and Fargo saddled the sturdy Ovaro. He mounted and turned the horse onto the main street. In a few minutes, Cedar City was behind them.

Overhead, the stars were bright in the clear night air. The rolling sage plain soon gave way to rugged country. The trail heaved up and down over the steep rills. The Ovaro, surefooted and hardy, galloped on, straining up the grades and taking the descents as if falling through the air, barely caught by its powerful legs. After two hours, the new moon rose, large and orange, fading to white as it climbed up the sky. Still Fargo rode on, his mind a quiet darkness, concentrating on the horse beneath him, on the rocky path, and on the sounds of the night. He kept a sharp eye out for anything off the trail. It was possible that once Frederico had got clear of town, he'd stopped for the night to sleep off the whiskey he'd been drinking. Possible, but not likely. Still, Fargo reasoned, it would be easy to miss the shape of a wagon pulled off in the darkness.

After three hours, Fargo became even more attentive to the night around him. Dawn was not far off. He'd calculated the speed of the wagon and the speed of the Ovaro. Any moment now, he figured, he'd be catching up to Frederico the Crooked Conjurer. Every time he galloped around a bend, he expected to see the decorated wagon just ahead. As the trail wound back and forth out of a steep arroyo, Fargo tried to imagine the loaded wagon straining up the slope. How fast could Frederico be driving that team? Surely he would come across him soon.

As the first blush of day spread across the east, Fargo mounted a rise and pulled the pinto to a halt. He gazed across the vast sage plain, which stretched for miles before him. He sat motionless as the sun slowly rose and the light poured across the flat, nubby table-land. If Frederico was out there, Fargo would see the wagon moving. His keen eyes swept the landscape, but he saw nothing. As the sun rose higher, the mead-owlarks rioted in the scrub, and still he sat, looking for a sign. Finally, he decided to give in to the suspi-cion that had been nagging him for hours—when the wily Frederico had asked the stable owner for direc-tions, it had been a ruse to throw any pursuer off the track. The anger rose in Fargo but quickly froze into the cold desire to find the thieving Frederico. He'd get the bald man eventually. He had no doubt of that. But he wouldn't underestimate Frederico again.

Fargo turned the Ovaro back in the direction of Cedar City. He put the horse into an easy canter. Thoughts of Hank Giffin and the trouble down in Mi-rage came into his mind. He had to get down to the Hopi land right away. Hank had said it was a matter of life and death. He'd have to explain to Arabella and Magnus that as soon as he took care of that, he'd come back to Cedar City and track down Frederico. But he knew the trail would be cold by then.

All the way back to town, Fargo kept his eyes open, in case he'd passed the wagon in the dark. But Fred-erico had escaped him.

It was late morning and the July sun had heated the thin air by the time he galloped into Cedar City. He returned the Ovaro to the stable with instructions for a full curry, water, and a bag of the best oats.

He found Magnus and his two daughters on the front porch of the boardinghouse. The gray-haired magician looked up hopefully as he spotted Fargo coming down the dusty street. "Any luck?" he asked.

Fargo shook his head and sat down wearily on a bench beside Arabella. Adrienne was hunched in a rocking chair, staring into the sun-blasted street. Magnus's face fell as Fargo told of the long night's ride on the trail to Denver City.

"So," Fargo finished, "I guess Frederico is smarter than I thought."

"Of course he is," Adrienne cut in. She held a flow-ered shawl tight around her, despite the heat of the day. Fargo looked at her closely. She was a dead ringer for Arabella, except for a small, dark mole on the left side of her mouth that gave her a slightly ex-otic look. She also had a sharp look about her dark eyes. "This never would have happened if you'd paid him what he was worth!" Adrienne shot at her father. "And now I'll never be Mrs. Connelly! I'll never get married! And it's all your fault!"

Magnus turned on her. "He was a lousy magician. Worthless. You just don't want to admit it because you fell in love with him. You still feel the same after he threatened me with a gun? And then stole all our equipment? I tell you, you're better off without him."

Adrienne jumped out of the chair, tears in her eyes. "It's not fair," she shouted at Magnus, but her voice had a tinge of doubt in it. "Poor Fred!" she exclaimed as she ran inside the house.

"Fred?" Fargo repeated, looking at Arabella with a smirk.

"Frederico's just his stage name," Arabella said.

Fargo felt the waves of exhaustion overtake him. It had been a long night's ride, and all for nothing. Frederico—Fred that is—was miles away by now. But in which direction? He could have gone north into Mormon country. Or he could have headed southwest along the Black Rock Trail. And meanwhile, Fargo should have been riding down the Piñon Trail, on his way to Mirage. He couldn't delay. But he knew after a long night on the trail he needed a few hours' rest before starting off.

"So, what now?" Magnus asked.

"After a nap, I've got to head down to Mirage," Fargo said. He explained all about the telegram and Hank Giffin. Magnus understood. "With luck, I'll be back in a week," Fargo added, his words almost slurred with exhaustion. "Then I'll find Frederico for you. I'm sorry I can't help you right now. But that's the way it is . . ."

The warmth of the morning sun relaxed him. He closed his eyes. If he could just rest against the wall for a few minutes . . . He felt Arabella get off the bench from beside him as sleep overtook him.

Voices and the creak of leather saddles awoke him sometime later. Fargo opened his eyes. Arabella sat in the rocking chair on the porch watching him. Magnus and Adrienne were nowhere to be seen. Fargo sat up and rubbed his stiff neck. Sleeping upright on a wooden bench was not one of his favorite pastimes, but he'd been too tired to even get up. The voices spoke again, rough voices. Two men dismounted in front of the boardinghouse and tethered their dusty mounts.

". . . a big old hot bath and a pretty woman," one of them, a rotund man with a red shirt, said. "Don't that sound great?"

"Yep," answered the other, a string bean of a man with a hangdog face. "I'll get these over to the stables," he added, gathering the reins and moving off with the two horses.

"You been on a hard ride?" Fargo asked amiably, rising, stretching, and stepping up to the railing.

"Sure have," the round one said, moving toward the porch. "Been in that goddamn saddle for twenty hours. And I've got a damn sore arse—" The man suddenly spotted Arabella on the porch and touched his hat to her. "Beg pardon, ma'am."

"Which way did you ride in?" Fargo asked. Maybe, just maybe, these men would have spotted Frederico.

"Up from the southeast," the man said. "On the Piñon Trail." Then he suddenly grew suspicious at the question. "What's all the questions? And who are you, anyway? Lawman, maybe?"

"Skye Fargo." The round man's eyebrows shot up.

"Famous guy. I've heard all about you, but I never thought I'd run into you. I'm Russ Blythe from Abilene. Why, just the other day . . . ."

"Never mind," Fargo said, cutting him off. This was no time for pleasantries. "Last night a man stole a wagon and rode out of Cedar City. I wonder if you'd have run into him. Bald fellow, mustache . . ." The man rubbed his chin in thought. "He was driving a tall enclosed wagon. Painted up with stars and a sign about a magic show."

"Oh, sure," Blythe said. "Sure, I know just the one you mean. Late last night we passed him. Most times you meet somebody on the trail at night, you stop and have a talk about what's up ahead. Not this fellow. He was tearing along at a good clip. Had a fine set of matched grays. But I didn't even get a peep at him."

"It has to be Frederico," Arabella said.

"Much obliged to you for the information," Fargo said as the man opened his mouth again. Russ Blythe clearly wanted to chat with the famous Trailsman, but Fargo took Arabella's arm. "Let's tell your father," he said, quickly ushering her inside. They found Magnus pacing back and forth in the parlor, a prim room with dark furniture and oil lamps with green glass globes. He was twisting his hands.

"I think we've got a lead," Fargo said. "Frederico's been spotted heading south on the Piñon Trail. That's the direction I'm riding."

"Marvelous!" Magnus said. "We'll just get some horses together and come with you."

"Not so fast," Fargo said. "For one thing, Frederico's moving at a gallop. This isn't going to be any leisurely ride. I don't think your daughters . . ."

"Just a minute, yourself," Arabella said hotly. "I'd like you to know that Adrienne and I are both excellent riders. Why, when we were little and Papa was part of a circus show, we were bareback riders! And—"

"Okay, okay!" Fargo said with a laugh, holding up his hands. "I'll get some horses over at the stable. How soon can you be ready?"

"Ten minutes!" Arabella called out over her shoulder as she hurried up the stairs. Fargo started to leave, but Magnus plucked at his sleeve.

"Mr. Fargo," the old magician said, "you know our money was taken, but I have some gold pieces here from our last show. For the horses. It's all we have left." Magnus dug in his pocket and held out some coins on his palm. Gold coins, about fifty dollars worth, Fargo saw. It wouldn't get them far.

"I'll take care of the horses," Fargo said. "And you can pay me back when we get Frederico."

"Thank you, Mr. Fargo. I won't forget this," Magnus said with a grateful smile. He balled up his fist around the gold pieces and instantly opened it again. The coins had vanished. Fargo laughed.

"Neat trick," he said.

Magnus grinned, showed his empty hand to Fargo, then brought it up to Fargo's ear and came away with one of the coins between his fingers.

"Too bad I can't really make money appear out of thin air," Magnus said sadly.

In a half hour, Fargo brought the four horses around to the front of the boardinghouse. He'd found a pair of matched chestnut fillies for Arabella and Adrienne, as well as a sturdy roan for Magnus. Each horse was outfitted with saddlebags packed with supplies Fargo had picked up at the general store, as well.

Arabella and Adrienne came out of the front door dressed in leather riding skirts and vests, with wide-brimmed hats to protect their faces against the harsh sun. They stowed a few personal items in their saddlebags and patted their horses. Magnus appeared in black from head to toe, the tall hat decorated with a silver brim made of stars.

"I'm going to set a fast pace," Fargo said, swinging into the saddle on the Ovaro. "But even so, it may be two or three days' hard ride to catch up to Frederico." He turned and watched as the two sisters easily mounted their chestnuts and sat tall in the saddles. Magnus nervously approached his roan and grunted as he lifted his short leg and inserted his toe into the stirrup. He tugged on the saddle horn and started to mount just as the horse took a faltering step sideways. Magnus, caught off balance, waved his arms in the air and toppled over, his foot still in the stirrup. Fargo jumped off the Ovaro and went over to help him up, hoping the roan wouldn't bolt and drag the old man down the street. A few passing pedestrians stopped to watch the sideshow.

"Lousy horse," Magnus said, dusting himself off.

"You ever ride before?" Fargo asked the old man as he adjusted the stirrup.

"My daughters are fine horsewomen," Magnus said hotly. He glanced at Fargo and then cleared his throat nervously. "I . . . ah, no. I always drive the wagon. But I'm sure it can't be that hard to ride one of these things."

Fargo held the roan steady as Magnus tried again. This time the horse stayed still, but the magician got stuck halfway up to the saddle. Fargo gave him a shove from behind and Magnus settled into the saddle.

"There," he said, straightening his hat and trying to look dignified. "This isn't so difficult. Now, to make him go, I just give him a little kick, isn't that right?"

Without waiting for an answer, Magnus dug his heels into the horse's ribs. The roan, startled and sensing the uncertainty of the rider on its back, reared and shot away at a hard gallop. Magnus, his elbows flapping, held on for dear life as the horse pounded down the street. Pedestrians and riders scurried out of the way. Arabella and Adrienne spurred their horses and chased after their father as Fargo ran to mount his Ovaro.

This was going to be a hell of a trip.

Four days later, Fargo stood at the top of a cliff, gazing across the valley several hundred feet below, where the shadows of clouds moved swiftly across a tumbled landscape of broken lava rock, scruffy gray-green sage, and buff grassland freckled by piñon pine. Far to the south, the high blue San Francisco peaks hid their heads in a bank of clouds. The late afternoon shadows lengthened in the pleats of the broken hills.

"You see him?" Arabella asked eagerly. "Can you see our wagon?"

Fargo reached out a hand and put it around Arabella's narrow waist, drawing her toward him. She laid her head on his shoulder.

"No," Fargo answered. "But that doesn't mean Frederico's not down there somewhere. Look over there," he pointed, "between those two dark hills. That's the town of Mirage. We'll be there by nightfall."

Fargo heard Adrienne's horse coming up the trail behind them. Magnus, he knew, was lagging behind, as he had all the way down the Piñon Trail. The old magician had had to learn to ride a horse the hard way, spending fourteen hours a day in the saddle.

Adrienne dismounted and joined them at the lookout point. She stood a distance away from them, shooting covert angry looks in their direction. Fargo, his arm still around Arabella's waist, ignored her. Adrienne had been out of sorts the whole journey. She was plainly jealous of Fargo's attention to her sister. And no doubt Adrienne was angry that her fiancé Frederico had turned out to be a louse and a thief. But she'd get over it, Fargo thought.

"That's the town of Mirage," Arabella said, pointing it out to her sister. Ever since Frederico had run off, Arabella had been making noticeable efforts to be nice to her sister. "That's where we're going."

A startled look passed over Adrienne's face, and she stared down at the dark ruffle of the few buildings visible between the distant hills.

"I know I've heard of the town of Mirage somewhere before," Arabella said. "Do you remember anything about it, Adrienne?"

Adrienne's face went stony. She shrugged and shook her head, then abruptly turned and walked back to her horse. Fargo watched her go. Something funny was going on, he thought. Adrienne knew something she wasn't telling. He wondered if it had to do with Frederico. That would make sense.

The roan cantered up the rise with Magnus clinging to its back, his hat blown back, gray hair flying everywhere, and a scowl on his sunburned face. He pulled the horse to a hard stop and slid down. He groaned as his boots hit the dirt. He staggered a step or two, then lowered himself onto a nearby rock, wincing.

"Nobody told me how much it hurts to ride a horse," the old man complained. "I hurt places I didn't even know I had."

"The better you ride, the better it feels," Fargo said. He glanced at the lowering sun. "But if we're going to get to Mirage by dark, we need to move on."

Magnus groaned and got slowly to his feet. Arabella stretched her lithe body before mounting again. Fargo watched her and thought for a moment of the time they'd spent on the trail. Each night, she'd left her tent and come to find him in his bedroll, out beneath the stars. And every long night had been a warm, fragrant savoring of one another as they found different ways to satisfy each other. There was a part of him that didn't want this trip to end. There was no telling what trouble lay ahead in Mirage. But he'd cabled Hank Giffin that he'd come to help. With the difficulty the old man had riding his roan, it had taken them longer than he'd hoped. Four days instead of three. But Frederico was bound to be down in Mirage. And Fargo couldn't wait to get his hands on him.

The town of Mirage—about a dozen board shacks—stood between two low hills at the eastern edge of the massive pine forest lying to the south and west that ran all the way to the San Francisco peaks. Here the trees petered out, and only cedars and piñons grew sporadically on the grassy slopes. As they rode down the trail toward Mirage, the low hills seemed to open up before them and Fargo could glimpse the land that lay to the east.

Beyond the town, the terrain sloped gradually downward and stretched out, seemingly to infinity. On that vast plain, there wasn't a tree in sight. Beyond Mirage, the Piñon Trail turned southward and hugged the hills, as if afraid to venture across that empty desert. The horizon, far away across the dusty expanse, was sharp with buttes and mesas against the darkening sky. It was all Hopi land, Fargo knew, scarred by the weird painted cliffs, eerie lines of cone hills, and sudden humps of red rocks that resembled gigantic turtles. Fargo had traveled that way before. The Hopi land was land that tested you—not just physically, but inside somehow.

But now his attention was drawn by a shout from the town up ahead. Someone had spotted them coming up the trail. Several figures hurried from the shacks, toting rifles. There was trouble, all right, Fargo thought. The whole town was on edge.

One man, tall with a weather-pitted face and iron-gray hair, stood out in front of the rest of the crowd of men, all waiting for their horses to draw near. Fargo was first to dismount.

"We don't get many strangers coming this way," the man said, still gripping his rifle. "Well, I'll be damned," he muttered, looking from Adrienne to Arabella and back again. "Excuse me, ladies. My name's Eben Blackwell. And who might you be?"

Fargo introduced himself, Magnus, and the two sisters. Blackwell stepped forward, relief on his craggy face. He pumped Fargo's hand and doffed his hat toward the twins.

"Well, well," Blackwell said. "The real Trailsman himself. Right here in Mirage. Ain't we lucky? Sun's almost down and you'll be needing a place to stay the night, won't you?"

Fargo withdrew his hand and got down to business. "I'm looking for two people," Fargo said. "First of all, a fellow named Frederico, the Fantastical Conjurer. He's a magician. He's driving a wagon all painted with stars. Would have come through in the last day or two. You seen him?"

Magnus started to cut in, but Fargo waved his hand to silence him. Blackwell scratched his head thoughtfully and turned around questioningly to the half-dozen men waiting behind him. They muttered among themselves.

"Nobody's come along the trail for a few days, at least," Eben said after a minute. "Couple of guys on horses, but they were heading to Cedar City. Last week we got a wagon of supplies up from the south," he said, brightening. "Maybe that's the guy?"

"No," Fargo said. Magnus looked crestfallen. Fargo wondered where the hell Frederico had gone. All the way along the trail, Fargo had seen the fresh deep ruts and cut earth of galloping hooves, but it had been impossible to be certain that the tracks had been made by Magnus's wagon of tricks. Nevertheless, the Piñon Trail wasn't much traveled, and Fargo's intuition told him that the fresh tracks had been Frederico's. Fargo cursed himself silently for not keeping a sharper eye out on the way into town. It had been several miles back that he had last noticed the tracks. The magician had clearly turned off somewhere back on the trail, but where? Fargo realized he'd have to retrace his steps and try to figure out where the wagon had gone. But it would have to wait until morning. Right now he had a promise to keep.

"I'm also looking for Hank Giffin," Fargo said. At the name, Eben Blackwell jumped.

"You a friend of his?" Blackwell asked, a strange note in his voice. His hands tightened on his rifle. The other men whispered among themselves and glanced warily at him. Fargo hesitated a moment before answering. He was reluctant to reveal what Hank had telegraphed to him—that there was trouble in Mirage. Maybe Eben Blackwell was mixed up in it. Fargo decided to play his cards close.

"I'm supposed to deliver something to him," Fargo said.

Blackwell gave him another look, head to toe, and then said in a low voice, "I'll take you to him." He turned and began walking toward one of the shacks. Fargo followed, while Magnus and his daughters brought up the rear. Blackwell turned around and waved his hand at the other three. "Just you, Fargo. The rest of you stay here."

Fargo hesitated for a moment. Was he walking into a trap? He didn't like the idea of leaving Magnus, Arabella, and Adrienne behind, unprotected, with the other men of Mirage. He couldn't tell yet exactly what was going on. Fargo drew Magnus aside for a moment and instructed him to take Arabella and Adrienne to wait by the horses and to ride out at the first sign of trouble. The three of them returned to the horses. Blackwell motioned Fargo to follow him as the other men drifted away into the shacks. They walked through the narrow, dusty streets of the tiny town and approached a crooked house with an open, gaping door. Fargo, resting his hand on the butt of his Colt, followed Eben Blackwell inside.

The interior of the shack was black, and Fargo caught the rustle of movement as Blackwell fumbled with something. In the close air of the cabin, Fargo picked up the odor he knew so well. Then a match was struck and the flame wavered toward an oil lamp sitting on a table nearby. Eben lit the wick and replaced the globe, turning up the light.

The golden glow slowly filled the room. And then Fargo saw what was left of Hank Giffin.

3

Hank Giffin lay on a long table, staring upward. His arms, outstretched in the shape of a cross and stiffened by rigor mortis, projected out beyond the edge of the table. Fargo slowly approached the table, taking shallow breaths against the stench. He could not tear his eyes away from Hank Giffin's hairy chest. Carved deep into the flesh was a triangle. Beneath it, a wavy line extended across his belly. Along the deep gouges in the flesh, the blood had blackened. Fargo motioned for Blackwell to bring the lamp nearer. He bent over the table and examined the markings.

"Who did it?"

"Must be Hopi," Blackwell said. "We've been lucky here so far. Haven't had any trouble with 'em. Maybe this is just the start of it. I found him this morning. He must have been out there for a day at least."

As Fargo stared at the strange markings, he noticed a small track, a kind of smudge leading up from the bloody triangle. The tiny marks, like small dots, marched in a line along Giffin's shoulder. He took the lamp from Blackwell and examined the markings painted onto the dead man's skin.

"Looks like little footprints," Fargo said. They

seemed to lead from Giffin's neck and hair down toward the pyramid. Fargo moved toward the corpse's head and saw that the entire top of the skull was a mass of dark, clotted blood. "Scalped?"

"That's what I thought at first," Blackwell said. Fargo could hear the man swallow hard before going on. "Actually, they took part of his skull, too. The whole top of his head's missing."

"Any ideas why?" Fargo said. "You had some trouble with the Hopis lately? Anybody been getting in their way?"

"Nothing like that," Blackwell said. "But Giffin, he'd been spending a lot of time out there with them . . ." Blackwell dug in his pocket and held a bandanna to his nose. "Do you mind if we step outside?"

Fargo doused the lamp and followed Blackwell out the door into the gathering dusk. Blackwell drew several deep breaths. They stood on the rickety porch.

"Did Hank say anything about what he was doing out there?" Fargo asked. Blackwell considered the question for a long moment.

"It's just real strange that the Hopis would kill Giffin. He was always one who liked the Indians," Blackwell said. "You know, they won't let most people near 'em. Last time I talked to Hank was about a week ago. He looked real worried. He said he'd discovered something that was going to cause a whole heap of trouble. And he was calling for some help. I asked him, What kind of trouble? You going to send for the U.S. Army? I said. But he said no, he was going to get some kind of special help."

Fargo examined Blackwell's rugged face in the last rays of sunset and decided he was telling the truth.

Whatever had happened to Hank Giffin out there, Blackwell had nothing to do with it.

"I guess I'm the help he sent for," Fargo said slowly. Blackwell looked at him with a start. "So whatever else you can tell me would help."

"Don't know much else," Blackwell said grimly. "Well, you'll be needing a place for the night. Given this killing, I wouldn't recommend camping out in the open around here. We've instituted a night watch on the town until we get to the bottom of this. But meanwhile, I've got a couple of extra beds over at my place. You and your friends are welcome to stay the night."

Blackwell made arrangements for their horses to be stabled and fed and then led them to his place, a rambling construction of a couple of gray board shacks connected together by some additions so new the lumber was still yellow. Blackwell ushered them inside a large central room furnished with heavy wooden tables and chairs, a huge stone fireplace, and colorful wool rugs on the floor and walls. He directed Magnus, Arabella, and Adrienne to some sparsely furnished bedrooms toward the back of the house so they could rest before supper. Then Blackwell rustled up some supper—a side of lamb, which he turned on a spit over the fire, as well as a mess of greens. Fargo sat on a stool by the fireplace, cleaning the trail dust from his Colt and Sharps rifle and oiling the mechanisms.

"Pretty women," Blackwell said, nodding toward the bedrooms where Arabella and Adrienne had gone. "Got lots of beaux, I guess." Fargo smiled to himself. He'd noticed Blackwell staring at Adrienne in particular.

"Adrienne's been engaged to that thieving magician," Fargo explained. He saw Blackwell's face fall and knew he'd guessed right. "But I think she'll get over it," he added and changed the subject. "Nice place you have here. How do you make a living out here in Mirage?"

"It's all sheep ranching hereabouts," Blackwell said, basting the sizzling mutton. "I got a herd I keep up in the hills. Good grass up there. Then in the winter, when it gets too cold, I have 'em brought down to the valley."

"On Hopi land?" Fargo asked, surprised.

"I hear tell the Indians don't mind it," Blackwell said with a shrug. "My herd's not so big and they don't wander far. Just the near grasslands. Once a year the wool's sent down the Piñon. And once a year we drive some mutton on the hoof across to Santa Fe or up north to Cedar City. The rest we sell hereabouts."

"Sounds like a good business. You hire men to herd for you?" Fargo asked.

"We've got an arrangement in Mirage that works out real well for us," Blackwell said as he scattered some dried rosemary on the roasting meat. "Every man in town has a herd branded with his mark. We board the flocks at the Circle C ranch, up in the hills west of here. It's Zeb Connelly's place." Fargo's mind raced. Connelly, Connelly. He'd heard that name somewhere recently. But where? Blackwell went on. "Zeb hires the herders. Twice a year, we all pitch in shearing and branding. Other than that, Zeb takes care of everything, and in exchange, we give him twenty percent."

Fargo sat and thought for a moment. If every man in town had a herd and all those sheep were grazing on Hopi land during the winter months, surely it

would antagonize the Indians. He wouldn't be sur-
prised if Hank's death had been a warning from the
Hopis. He thought again about the mutilation of
Hank's body.

"Any idea what those carvings on Giffin's chest
meant?" Fargo asked.

"I don't read Hopi pictures," Blackwell said with a
shrug. Then he glanced at Fargo, his face bright with
an idea. "But one of Zeb's herders is a Hopi. Fellow
by the name of Running Dog. Maybe he could tell
you."

"I think I'll ride up there tomorrow," Fargo said. He
had to track Frederico's wagon anyway, he thought.
And maybe the men at the ranch would have seen the
stolen wagon.

Arabella emerged from the back rooms, having
changed into a rose-colored dress that clung to her
curves and accentuated her tiny waistline and high
breasts. Her loosened hair tumbled over her shoulders
like gleaming cascades of black water and she looked
rested and refreshed. She smiled at Fargo's appreciative glance and helped Blackwell finish the dinner
preparations. Magnus and Adrienne appeared soon afterward, the old magician limping from his four-day
ordeal in the saddle. They took their places at the
table and Blackwell dished up a delicious meal. He
was especially solicitous of Adrienne, Fargo noted.

Afterward, Magnus, looking more relaxed, pulled a
deck of cards from his vest pocket and began to shuffle them.

"You a gambling man?" Blackwell asked as Magnus deftly flicked the cards in a perfect waterfall from
one palm to the other. The magician's eyes twinkled.
He fanned the cards and presented them to Blackwell.

"Pick one," he said. "But don't show it to me."

Blackwell hesitated a moment, looking in confusion at Fargo.

"Magician," Fargo said. Blackwell grinned and picked a card from the center, careful that no one would see the face. He glanced at it and returned it to the deck. Magnus snapped the cards into a pile and handed it to Blackwell.

"Cut and shuffle them," Magnus said. Blackwell did so, then laid the pile in the center of the table. Magnus tapped the cards three times and said some incomprehensible words and then turned over the top card.

Blackwell stared. "Goddamn," he said with a disbelieving laugh. "Four of hearts. Damn right. Goddamn. You know any more tricks like that?"

Magnus grinned and shook his head while he showed his empty hand to Blackwell. Then he made a fist and with the other hand began pulling a red silk handkerchief from it, which was knotted to a blue one, a yellow one, a green one, and an orange one. Blackwell chuckled.

"I bet the rest of the fellows would like to see this," he said. "You mind if I call them in?" In answer, Magnus rose from his chair and reached under the table to bring up a bouquet of silk flowers.

"We would be honored to do a few simple demonstrations of the art of magic for the good citizens of Mirage," Magnus intoned. Fargo grinned at the sound of Magnus's voice—the booming, stagey voice he remembered from the magic show had returned. The old magician's eyes gleamed and his face shone.

Within a half hour, almost everyone who wasn't on guard duty assembled in Blackwell's great room. For the next hour, Magnus and his daughters pulled flowers out of thin air, coins from ears and empty glasses, and made cards disappear and reappear in the most unlikely places. The citizens of Mirage—all men, since the town was deemed too rugged and raw for women and children—were a good audience. They shouted and stamped at every trick and whistled appreciatively at the two women. At the conclusion of the show, Fargo passed around his hat and they threw in a few dollars. After everyone had gone, Magnus sat at the table to count the money.

"Not bad," Magnus said with a delighted cackle as he stacked the last coin. "Maybe we should play these small towns more often." His face, which looked younger than it had for days—since the wagon had been stolen—suddenly darkened again. "But if I don't get my devices back," he added, "I'll never play the big cities again." He shook his head sadly and rose. He and Adrienne retired for the evening. Blackwell yawned and said good night. Only Arabella lingered, waiting by the red-ember fire.

"You ready for bed?" she asked, glancing up at Fargo shyly.

"I'm going out for a look around," Fargo said, pulling her toward him. His mouth found her warm lips and his tongue flicked inside them. He let her go reluctantly. "I'll be back soon." Fargo took his Colt, unlatched the door, and let himself out into the darkness.

Even in summer, nights were chilly on the desert. Fargo buttoned his buckskin jacket. He didn't know what he expected to find, but he wanted to get a good look at the town of Mirage. And besides, he felt cooped up if he stayed inside too long.

The gritty dust whispered under his boots as he made his way down the street. Golden lamplight shone through the windows and chinks in some of the shacks. Sparks flew into the clear, star-studded sky from a chimney at one end of the street. He found the stable and went in to check on the Ovaro. He found his black-and-white pinto in one of the stalls, well supplied with oats and fresh water. He let himself out of the stable and made his way to the edge of town, where the Piñon Trail led back toward Cedar City.

"Halt!" a deep voice called out from behind a piñon pine nearby. Fargo heard the click of a rifle. He quickly identified himself. "Oh, okay," said the voice as the man stepped out from behind a tree and approached him. In the dim starlight, Fargo recognized a short, pudgy man he'd seen when they rode in. "We're all taking turns guarding the town tonight," the man explained. "Just in case those Hopis try a sneak attack."

The possibility seemed unlikely to Fargo, first of all because Indians rarely, if ever, attacked at night, usually preferring dawn. And second, because Hopis weren't the attacking kind. But still, it was better to be careful. Fargo exchanged a few words with the man and stood for a while listening to the quiet sigh of the night wind through the cedars and piñons on the hills west of town. Frederico was up there somewhere, Fargo thought. And tomorrow he'd find him.

After a few minutes, Fargo said good night and headed back to Blackwell's. He'd just come in sight of the shack where Hank Giffin's body lay when his keen eyes caught a faint movement in the shadows up ahead. Fargo quickly stepped aside and into the darkness alongside a rickety abandoned hut. He pressed himself against the wooden wall and waited, stilling his breath, his eyes and ears alert.

The street was still. He caught the faint sound of voices from inside a house down the street, and then a clatter of pans. A few houses over, a door slammed shut. He continued to wait, watching the hut holding Giffin's corpse until he wondered if he had been wrong. But then he saw it. Inside the hut, a light suddenly flickered and then was extinguished. A moment later came another movement and the whisper of gravel underfoot. A dark figure slipped out of the shack and hurried away. Silently drawing his Colt and hunching low, Fargo ran forward in pursuit. The figure disappeared between two dark houses. When Fargo got to the spot, he looked down the empty street, which led to the eastern edge of town and overlooked the wide desert. Moving warily, he walked forward, scanning to the right and left between the buildings in case whoever it was had taken cover between them. When he reached the edge of Mirage, he heard a movement from the darkness of an overhanging porch. Fargo's finger tightened on the trigger. Once again a voice called out for him to stop. Fargo identified himself as the man on guard duty came forward.

"I spotted somebody sneaking around," Fargo said. "Did he come this way?"

"N–n–no," the skinny man stuttered. "I sure didn't see anyone." He looked around nervously. "What did . . . did he look like? Was it an Indian?"

"Too dark to tell," Fargo answered. "But he moved like a shadow."

Fargo left the nervous watchman and for the next half hour walked back and forth between the buildings, looking and listening for any sign of the mysterious figure. But he saw nothing. When Fargo had finally given up all hope of finding him, he decided to check on Giffin's corpse. What had the man been doing in the hut anyway?

Fargo entered, Colt in hand, and struck a match, holding it high. The momentary flare of light showed him what he needed to see. Hank Giffin still lay on the table, but resting on his chest, across the bloody marks, was an eagle feather. The match burned out. Fargo walked back to Blackwell's, his thoughts whirling.

Whoever had gone into the hut had lit a match, just as Fargo had just done, in order to see Hank Giffin's body. And he'd left an eagle feather and run away. But who was it? And why had he left the feather?

Fargo suddenly felt weary as he remembered Hank Giffin—a good man, a good soldier. Hank had been killed because he'd found out something. Something about the Hopis. Something dangerous. And Fargo was determined to find out what it was. No matter what the cost.

Dawn glowed rosy in the window when Fargo got out of bed and dressed. He stood buckling on his holster and looking down at Arabella as she lay asleep on her side in the tangle of sheets, her dark hair strewn over the pillow and her ripe, round breasts visible above the top of the sheet. Every night it seemed to get better between them, as their familiarity with each other's bodies grew; and yet there were always new things to explore. He smiled and leaned over to kiss the silken skin of her shoulder. Arabella stirred and her eyelids fluttered.

"Skye?" she murmured. She came awake as she realized he was up and dressed. "Is there something wrong?"

"I'm heading up to the hills," he said. "Looking for Frederico. And I'll also visit a sheep ranch up there. You'll be safe here with Blackwell. Just make sure your father gets some rest."

Arabella pretended to pout until he kissed her, then she laughed and wrapped her arms around his neck.

"I hope you never find Frederico," she whispered in his ear. Then she grew serious. "I don't really mean that."

"I know what you mean," Fargo said with a smile. He slipped the Colt in his holster and headed out to the stable.

A half hour later, he was cantering over the Piñon Trail. The Ovaro kicked up its heels, happy to be out of the stable and in the open again. The clear dome above them promised a hot day ahead, but Fargo knew the big sky was deceiving in this country. On most summer afternoons, dark clouds would appear in the west by early afternoon, bringing a violent thunderstorm but only a spatter of rain.

As the sun rose higher, the jays chattered raucously in the cedars. The first thing he had to do was to find where Frederico had turned off the trail. Fargo kept his eyes on the hard-packed earth. He'd gone five miles along the trail, but it was marked only with hoofprints and wagon ruts too old to be Frederico's. He neared the foot of the high red lookout cliff, where the trail was rocky, and slowed the pinto to a walk in order to examine the broken ground more carefully. Then he saw what he'd been looking for. Fargo dismounted and examined the tracks. There was no question—the ruts of the wagon wheels appeared and reappeared in the dusty ground between the patches of gravel and broken rock. But a grassy patch beside the trail was scored deep by fresh parallel tracks that led due south across open grassland in the direction of a low saddle between two hills.

Fargo swung onto the pinto and followed the ruts up the gently sloping meadow, over the saddle, through a gorge, and onto a high, flat plateau surrounded by higher hills. The tracks continued due south for another mile across the grassland and then ran straight into a dirt road. Fargo stopped the Ovaro as he gazed at the ribbon of bald earth that cut through the grass and led at either end into the hills. The wide road was scored deep by the tracks of many different wagon wheels and horses' hooves, some very recent, going in both directions. It was impossible to discern which way Frederico had gone and which tracks were his. Fargo retraced his steps and examined the wagon tracks in the grass leading to the road, trying to determine if the wagon had angled either direction as it approached the road. He thought the tracks curved slightly east, indicating that Frederico had turned onto the road in that direction, but it was impossible to be certain. Nonetheless, he decided to go a few miles and see what was up there.

It was nearing noon and he had galloped only a couple of miles into the piñon-covered hills when he came on a sign burned into a big wooden plank. CIRCLE C RANCH—NO TRESPASSING, it read. Fargo ignored it and rode on. As the road snaked over a few low hills, he heard the bleating of sheep and soon came on a huge herd, a gently rolling sea of dirty white backs, grazing in a stubby meadow. Sheep were voracious eaters and unlike cattle pulled up the roots of the grasses. A herd of sheep needed a lot of land. He looked about for sheepherders, but saw no one. He was just plunging down a slope when without warning a rifle shot whizzed over his head. The sheep bleated and skittered to the other side of the meadow at the sound of the gunfire. The shot had come from the direction of a clump of rocks and dark cedars just ahead. Fargo reined in the Ovaro immediately and waved his hands above his head.

"Hey! I'm a friend of Eben Blackwell! In Mirage!"

There was a long silence and then a tall, skinny man stepped out from behind the rocks, his rifle still aimed at Fargo.

"Ride closer," he yelled. "But keep your hands in the air."

Fargo did as he was told. Most ranchers were touchy about who rode onto their land, he thought, but this was ridiculous. As he neared, the skinny man squinted at him.

"Now, who are ya?"

"Skye Fargo. I'm staying with Eben Blackwell."

The skinny man relaxed a shade, but didn't lower his rifle. "So?"

"So," Fargo said, stalling for time as he looked the man over. He didn't like him. If the ranch was this well guarded, then something fishy was going on. Fargo wondered if word of Hank Giffin's murder had reached the Circle C yet. He decided he'd start with Frederico first and see where that got him. "I've been tracking a man from Cedar City," Fargo said, slowly lowering his hands.

"What kind of man?"

"A guy by the name of Frederico the Conjurer. A

magician. Made off with somebody else's wagon. Kind of a fancy painted thing. You seen anybody around here like that?"

The other man's eyes never left Fargo's, but they narrowed.

"No," he said, with a note of anger in his voice. "I ain't seen nobody around here like that."

"Well . . ." Fargo began, looking off into the distance. The man was lying. Unmistakably. "Maybe one of the other men spotted him. I'll just ask at the ranch house and . . ." Fargo picked up his reins as if to ride on, and the skinny man took a step forward, tightening his grip on the rifle.

"Look, stranger, this is a private ranch," the man said. "You know what's good for you, you get outta here. Now." He tightened his finger on the trigger.

There was no arguing with a rifle, Fargo thought. He shrugged and was about to turn the Ovaro back when he heard the sound of horses approaching from the direction of the ranch. The skinny man heard it, too, and looked up expectantly. In a moment, a dozen riders swept over the rise. In their lead and mounted on a magnificent ebony stallion was a tall man dressed all in gray. He slowed when he spotted Fargo and brought the group forward at a walk.

"Bill? Who is this?" the tall man asked. His smooth face was composed of hard planes, as if it were a faceted rock. A close-clipped gray mustache marked his upper lip and a huge ring of keys jangled at his belt. Under his deep hat brim, his intelligent eyes glittered.

"Says his name's Skye Fargo," Bill said, keeping his rifle trained on Fargo.

"Oh, the famous Trailsman," the man in gray said

with interest. He searched Fargo with his eyes. "What brings you to the Circle C?"

"You must be Zeb Connelly," Fargo said. "Eben Blackwell told me I'd find you up here. I've got some questions."

"Put your rifle down, Bill," Zeb said smoothly. "We should be more welcoming to our famous guest. Now, Mr. Fargo, what kind of questions?"

"He's looking for . . ."

Zeb held up his hand and gave Bill a sharp look.

"Silence! I'm sure Mr. Fargo can tell me himself." Zeb waved his arm grandly. "Welcome to the Circle C, Mr. Fargo. Come to the ranch house and join us for our midday meal."

"But he's . . . ." Bill cut in, sounding almost panicky. Fargo wondered what was going on. Zeb cut off the man again.

"That's enough, Bill," Zeb said. "Ride ahead to the ranch house and take care of things. Tell Juan to set an extra place for lunch."

Bill's long face brightened and he turned on his heel and went to retrieve his horse, which was hidden in the cedars. In another moment, he was galloping down the road.

"And the rest of you, go take care of the matter of that straying herd." The other men moved off down the road. "Now, Mr. Fargo," Zeb said, turning his chiseled face toward him, "before we get down to business, how about a tour of the ranch?"

For the next half hour, Fargo followed as Zeb rode along the hills and through the broad meadows of the Circle C, which spread up into the hills. In places, the grass was patchy and the bare earth showed where the sheep had overgrazed, but other meadows were luxuriant with waving yellow stalks. Zeb pointed out the various herds belonging to different men in Mirage and then led the way to the ranch headquarters. At the bottom of a grassy bowl stood a collection of low log buildings set among a maze of holding pens and corrals. A large barn stood to one side, the doors closed. They dismounted in front of the largest log building and tethered their horses. Zeb led the way in, removed his hat, and ran a hand through his gray, thinning hair.

The huge room was dominated by a fireplace big enough to roast a whole buffalo in. A long wooden table, which could have accommodated twenty, was set for three. Bill sat squirming in his chair. Fargo smiled at the skinny man as he took the place indicated by Zeb.

"So, Bill," Fargo said in a friendly voice, "how long have you worked at the Circle C?"

Bill shot a glance at Zeb before answering. "Been here five years," he said defensively.

Juan, a small, dark man with liquid brown eyes, appeared with steaming plates of food. As he was putting them on the table, Zeb addressed Fargo. "So, you said you had some questions. Please."

Fargo repeated what he'd said to Bill about Frederico. At the sound of the man's name, Juan dropped a plate on the table. It broke and scattered a stack of tortillas across the tabletop. He muttered excuses in Spanish, swept the bread and shards of pottery off the table, and retreated into the kitchen. Fargo took this all in but kept his eyes on Zeb. Juan was nervous about something and it had to do with Frederico. The planes of Connelly's face never so much as moved.

Meanwhile, Bill shoveled beans into his mouth, his eyes on his plate.

"And you think this . . . this road-show magician came this direction?" Zeb said. "I'm afraid you're mistaken, Mr. Fargo. My men would have seen him if he had." He paused a moment, his eyes thoughtful. "A thief wouldn't drive straight into a ranch. He would have headed the other direction on that road."

And how would Frederico know which way to go? Fargo wondered, but he kept his thoughts to himself. "Just where does that road go?" Fargo asked.

"It leads around through the hills and circles back to join the Piñon Trail south of town. The terrain's less rugged that way. Fewer inclines. That's why we never cut a road over the hills the way you rode in."

Fargo realized he wasn't going to find out anything more about the vanished magician. It was possible that Frederico had headed the other direction on the road, which would have taken him back to the Piñon Trail and bypassed the town. Somehow Fargo couldn't shake the feeling that Zeb and Bill knew more than they were telling. But asking more questions about Frederico wasn't going to get him anywhere. As he ate, Fargo turned over the business about Hank Giffin in his mind. When Blackwell told him that the Circle C sheep were grazing on Hopi land, Fargo had thought that might be the key to the Hopis having killed Giffin. But now he wondered if it was that simple. He glanced up at Zeb and found the rancher watching him, as if reading his thoughts.

"So, the sheep graze up here in the hills during the summer," Fargo said. Juan arrived with another plate of hot tortillas, which he set carefully down on the table. He glanced curiously at Fargo and then left the room.

"It's cooler up here in the hills," Zeb said, passing him the tortillas. "Then in the winter, we drive the herds to the bottomlands."

"That's Hopi land," Fargo pointed out blandly. "They don't mind?"

Zeb looked at him sharply. "You must have heard about that unfortunate murder in Mirage," the rancher said. "That fellow—what was his name? Oh, yes, Hank Giffin. Look, we've never had any trouble with the Hopi because we treat 'em right. They don't mind us grazing because we give them plenty of mutton and wool in exchange for the land use. Why, I've even got one of those Hopis working here on the ranch." Zeb paused a moment, his eyes fixed on Fargo. "No, Mr. Fargo, somebody put the wrong idea in your head. The murder of Hank Giffin doesn't have to do with grazing. It's a religious killing."

Zeb took a slow sip of his coffee as the words hung in the air. Religious killing, Fargo thought. What could that possibly mean? He'd never heard of any such thing attached to the mysterious Hopi beliefs. On the other hand, the Hopis kept their religion so secret that maybe Zeb was right.

"I heard the Hopis had carved some pictures in Giffin's corpse," Zeb said. Fargo nodded assent. "Well, that proves it."

"It doesn't prove anything," Fargo said. The rancher shrugged.

They had finished eating and Fargo decided it was time to go. There was a lot unsaid between him and Zeb. And it looked like it was going to stay that way. He didn't like the imperious rancher and it was clear the feeling was mutual. Fargo rose and reached for his hat. "Thanks for the hospitality," he said stiffly. "I'll see myself out."

"Go with him, Bill," Zeb said. He turned and left the room, the keys jangling at his belt with each step and his boot heels a loud staccato on the wooden floor.

Outside, Fargo untethered the pinto and was about to mount when he spotted a group of ranch hands striding toward the big house. One of them in particular caught his attention.

"Hey! Running Dog!" Fargo called out, remembering the name of the Hopi ranch hand Blackwell had mentioned the night before. At the sound of his name, the small Indian man looked up. He was dressed in Levi's and a plaid shirt like the other ranch hands. His features were small and his eyes piercing. Suspicion crossed Running Dog's face. Fargo approached the group.

"Zeb told me you're Hopi," Fargo said. "I wonder if you can help me with something."

Fargo picked up a stick from the ground and drew a triangle with a wavy line beneath it. Leading from it, he dug a small trail of dots upward from the pyramid shape. Running Dog, his face twisted into an expression that Fargo couldn't read, stared down at the ground and then looked up at him angrily.

"Why are you drawing these pictures?" Running Dog asked, sweeping his boot over the marks to obliterate them.

"It's Hopi writing. What does it mean?" Fargo persisted.

"You don't have to tell him nothing," Bill cut in hotly.

Running Dog ignored him.

"These signs are supposedly made by *kachina* spirits," Running Dog said to Fargo defiantly. "Ghosts. That is the picture of the Red City of my ancestors. It is where the sun goes in the winter. Many moons that way." He gestured toward the south. "The sacred river runs underneath."

"And those dots? They looked like footprints."

"Enough!" Running Dog said impatiently. He turned and marched away angrily. Fargo watched him go.

"It's a message that the Hopi are supposed to go to the Red City," Bill said slowly. Fargo glanced at him. "I've heard Running Dog say that," he added. Then he glanced around, as if he had said too much. The ranch hands moved away uncomfortably, and Bill, with a backward glance, disappeared into a nearby stable. Fargo returned to his Ovaro and prepared to mount. Just then, he saw a curtain flicker at a window of the big house. He wondered if Zeb Connelly had been watching. Sudddenly, Fargo heard a sound—his name being called, but softly, urgently. He spotted the cook, Juan, crouched on one side of the big log house. The little man was gesturing for him to come over. With a glance around to make sure no one was watching, Fargo walked quickly over to Juan.

"I heard you . . ." Juan said, struggling to make himself understood in English, ". . . make question about the . . ." He struggled for the word. "*Magico.*"

"The magician. Frederico," Fargo said hastily. "Have you seen him?"

"*Sí! Sí!*" Juan said excitedly, his brown eyes darting. "I have seen . . ."

"What's going on here?" Zeb's sharp voice rang

out. Juan jumped and whirled about. The tall rancher stood at the corner of the log house watching them, fury on his face.

"I left my hat on the table," Fargo said easily. He tapped it for emphasis. "Your man was just returning it to me." Juan muttered in Spanish and hastily retreated behind the back of the house, looking guilty as hell.

"Good try, Trailsman," Zeb said, ice in his voice. "But you left the table with your hat on. Now, get off my ranch."

Fargo turned away with a silent curse. Hell, he hoped Zeb hadn't heard Juan's words. So, Frederico had been spotted on the ranch. But where was he? And why were Zeb and his men lying about it? As he mounted the Ovaro, Fargo hoped Zeb wouldn't wreak revenge on the little cook. If he had another chance, Fargo thought, he'd try to get a word with Juan.

As he mounted the pinto, Fargo saw Bill emerge from the stable with a horse. Fargo mounted the Ovaro and rode off. All the way to the border of the ranch, Bill followed him. Once past the boundary of the Circle C, Fargo put the Ovaro into a gallop along the road, which led up a gentle rise. At the top, he glanced back. Bill sat on his horse, watching.

Fargo continued along the road, which circled the hills and returned eventually to join the Piñon Trail, south of Mirage. The early afternoon sun was hidden behind an advancing wall of gray clouds. Fargo heard the boom of distant thunder as he followed the trail, doubling back in a broad loop to head due east. Fargo put the Ovaro in an easy lope as they passed through the miles of territory. Much of the grassland, tucked in between the forests of pine and cedar, showed the ravages of sheep grazing.

Coming around a bend in the trail, he spotted an approaching supply wagon, with several outriders, coming from the opposite direction. The riders gave him hard looks as they galloped by. Otherwise, he saw no one. Once, a rain shower spattered the dust but passed quickly. When he reached the Piñon Trail, which skirted the foot of the hills, Fargo dismounted and examined the tracks in the earth. As he feared, there were the marks of many wagons, some turning north for the short trip into Mirage and others turning south for the long trek eastward to Santa Fe.

He let the Ovaro graze for a while on the short grass near the trail as he pondered what to do next. To the east lay the seemingly endless expanse of Hopi lands. The grassland sloped gradually downward for miles until it reached the dry desert bottom, broken here and there by buttes and painted cliffs. In the distance was a massive orange mesa, still in full sun. Above him were rain clouds, angry and black. Occasional thunder rumbled and cracked like splitting rocks. The shadow of the cloud bank, moving west, was slowly slipping over the broad land.

As Fargo gazed across the darkening terrain, he thought he spotted movement out among some rocks that rose like a red tower in the middle of a salt flat. Fargo fixed his eyes on the spot and saw it again. Something moving, something that didn't belong on the land, something amiss. It was several miles away and impossible to identify, but Fargo felt instinctively that there was something out there he needed to know about.

He mounted the pinto and rode slowly down the

grassy slope into the land of the Hopis. As he left the shelter of the hills behind him, the expanse of land before him and around him seemed to open up to take him in. When he had gone a mile, he paused to look back at the hills, which suddenly seemed formidable. As he rode forward again, he sighted the finger of rock, the red tower he had glimpsed from above. He headed toward it, the Ovaro's hooves alternately sinking into the fine-grained sand of the alkali flats and clattering on the patches of brown scree that littered the desert floor. As he neared the rock promontory, Fargo slowed the pinto and became wary. The clouds reverberated overhead, but no rain fell. A hot wind blew from the west.

The bunchgrass ended at the edge of the wide white flat on which stood the pointing rock, surrounded by a scattering of huge red boulders. He halted the Ovaro and sat looking at the mammoth pillar rising into the sky before him. There it was again. Painted on the rock face in white—the triangle, the wavy line, and a sinuous trail of footprints leading to them. Then his ears caught a slight sound. A sharp cracking. Something flapping in the wind.

Following the sound, he rode forward a few paces until the source of the noise came into view. He saw several stakes with animal skins tied to them driven into the ground in a semicircle. The skins danced wildly in the strong wind, which also kicked up the dust around him. That was the movement he'd seen from up in the hills. But now the shape of something else lying on the ground drew him. He walked the Ovaro forward another hundred yards, dismounted, and, Colt in hand, drew near until he stood over it.

The Hopi had been dead for hours. His arms were

thrown outward as Giffin's had been. And the same macabre symbols—the pyramid of the Red City and the waving sacred river—had been cruelly carved into the flesh. Footprints had been drawn on the skin, too, and once again the top of the head was a bloody mass of crushed and missing skull.

A bolt of lightning suddenly exploded above, throwing an eerie flash of light over the rocks. The earsplitting thunder followed a moment later. He should get the pinto to cover. Just then, he spotted movement around him.

A tall Hopi brave stepped out from behind a rock, a long knife in his raised hand. Then Fargo saw a second Indian materialize from behind another boulder. Then another and another. A second flash of lightning lit the scene and the thunder roared. Fargo was surrounded on all sides by a dozen silent Hopi braves, each armed with a knife.

"You are not the *kachina* spirit," the tall brave said in clear English. He raised his glittering knife. "Why do you pretend to be *kachina*? Why are you killing my people?"

The warriors took a step toward Fargo just as the lightning struck again.

4

The lightning exploded, the fiery bolt crackling down from the black clouds above and striking the top of the tall red rock. For a fiery instant, it appeared that the rock tower dangled from the sky above in a ragged path of white light that flashed and danced. Immediately, the thunder roared, a deafening crack followed by a rolling boom echoed by the rocks and clouds. Fargo felt his hair standing on end with the electricity in the air.

All around him, the Hopi braves cowered, hugged the ground, and looked fearfully toward the sky. Only Fargo and the tall brave remained standing. The black cloud above rumbled and flashed again as a bolt jumped within the cloud, from one billowing arm to the next. A few hot raindrops spattered the dust.

"Maybe you are *kachina*," the Hopi said, lowering his knife slightly. He glanced at the corpse of the brave lying between them on the ground. His eyes narrowed.

"This man has been dead since the sun rose," Fargo said, remembering words of the Hopi dialect, similar to that spoken by the Utes and Comanche. The brave seemed startled to hear his own language. It was obvious to Fargo that the Hopis had no idea who had killed this brave. And from what the Indian had said, Fargo guessed that the killings had happened before.

"I did not kill this brave," Fargo explained. "And I am no more *kachina* than you are. My name is Skye Fargo. By my people I am called the Trailsman. The Apaches named me Silver Wolf. To the Cheyenne, I am Seeing Eagle, and to the Blackfoot, I am Running Elk. I have many other names as well."

Fargo finished and was silent for a moment. The formal telling of names was an important courtesy among most Indians. The Hopi brave looked at him carefully for a long moment. All around them, the other Indians got slowly to their feet. The clouds above, while still flashing with light, were moving swiftly to the east in the stiff wind. A light rain fell on them and hissed across the sand.

"I am Sun-Sky of the Badger clan," the brave said. He looked down again at the dead man, then raised his hand. Two braves came forward and lifted the mutilated body, carrying it away behind a rock. Then, as if they had never spoken, Sun-Sky turned away from Fargo. All the Hopis began leaving, disappearing swiftly between the rocks as mysteriously as they had come. Fargo started to call after Sun-Sky, but decided he would simply follow. There was too much he needed to know. Fargo walked behind Sun-Sky, turning once to whistle at the Ovaro, which followed along after him.

On the other side of the rocks, they came to a small culvert where the Hopis had hidden their horses. The young boy who was guarding them looked fearfully at Fargo as he walked up, then tore his gaze away. The Hopis mounted, as did Fargo. None of the Indians looked at him, except for the boy, who stole curious glances. The Indians rode in a close pack away from the red-rock tower, with Fargo following at a respectful distance.

For the next hour, he trailed the Hopis as they galloped over the rugged terrain, which changed dramatically with each passing mile, from the salt flats scarred by dusty-red outcroppings to patches of waving grass spotted with black lava boulders to smooth, barren hills of ashen soil striped with violet, yellow, and pink. Soon they drew near a massive orange cliff, carved by the relentless wind into a hundred twisted and fantastical faces. As they galloped straight toward the huge wall of rock, it loomed higher and higher above them.

At the base of the cliff, Fargo spotted the dark square form of a building sitting on a wide meadow of buff grass. The riders veered off and Fargo, following them, got a close look as he galloped by. The log shack was dilapidated, with empty, staring windows and a stove-in roof. The bars of the corral had been busted and the water trough had collapsed. Fargo wondered who had tried to build a ranch in such lonely country and what had happened to him.

They rode by a clear spring that bubbled up from the cliff and ran a short way before disappearing again into the dry desert earth. Then the pack of Hopis rounded the mesa and slowed their horses to a walk as they began to climb a narrow, rocky switchback trail. Only once, when a stumbling Hopi horse dislodged a shower of loose stones, did Sun-Sky turn around to make sure that Fargo was still with them. If they didn't want him tagging along, Fargo reasoned, they'd have stopped him. But Hopis weren't ones for wasting words.

Finally, the horses climbed the last rise and came out on top of the mesa. The broad sky was spread above. The afternoon storm had drifted to the east and the sky was bright in the west over the hills. At one end of the mesa stood the jumbled box shapes of an adobe pueblo. Fargo knew the Hopi did not often let strangers come to their dwelling place. At the edge of the pueblo, everyone dismounted.

Now Sun-Sky motioned for Fargo to follow. Fargo turned and handed the reins of his Ovaro to the young boy, who stared at Fargo with large black eyes and then looked appreciatively at the black-and-white pinto. The boy stroked the horse's rippling, muscular flank with a pleased smile. The pinto, feeling the boy's sure hand, turned its magnificent head to nuzzle him.

"You are strong like a bear, wise like the moon," the boy whispered to the horse. Fargo smiled to himself. He had no doubt the boy would pamper his faithful pinto.

Sun-Sky led the way among the adobe buildings. Fargo heard his names being whispered from one to another of the passing Hopis. Women carrying water baskets stared at him and giggled. Fargo noticed one in particular, a lithe beauty in a blue-beaded buckskin dress who sat weaving at a loom in the sheltering shade of a wall. He smiled at her as he passed. She returned the smile and boldly called out to Sun-Sky to ask who the white man was. Sun-Sky ignored her question until they were out of sight.

"That is Raindrop, wife of Black Crow," Sun-Sky explained. "He was the first to be killed, and she waits one more moon until another man can come forward to marry her. She is not supposed to speak and men are not supposed to speak to her. But she is wild like the deer. No one can tell Raindrop what to do."

Soon they came to a ladder resting against a high, curved wall. They ascended and Fargo realized he was being taken into the *kiva*, the sacred meeting room where the men met for religious rituals and to make the important decisions for the tribe.

They descended a second ladder through a sky hole into the round room. As Fargo's eyes adjusted to the gloom, he saw rows of braves sitting against the thick adobe walls. They whispered to each other as they looked him over. A small fire burned in the center of the large room and the smoke rose through the round hole in the ceiling. The *kiva* was cool and dark, the dirt floor hard and swept clean. It smelled of woodsmoke and herbs. Sun-Sky sat and pointed to a spot next to him and Fargo sat. After a few minutes of silence, an old man, his long white hair loose over his shoulders, started chanting. Fargo knew most of the words—it was a prayer-song about eagle feathers and the Humpbacked Flute Player, who scattered seeds from his hump. After a while, the old man stopped singing and Sun-Sky spoke.

"My father," the young brave said, addressing the old man, "your *kataimatoqve*, your invisible sun-eye, saw the truth. I found one of our braves, Green Corn Standing. He had the marks of the Red City on him. He walks with the *kachina* spirits now."

"Who is this white man?"

"He is the Wanderer," Sun-Sky said, a note of excitement in his voice. "The one white men call the Trailsman. We have heard the stories of him from our brothers in the west. This is a good sign."

"Maybe," the old man said. "But what if he, this

78

Wanderer, is two-hearted?" Fargo had heard the Hopis use the words two-hearted to mean someone who could not be trusted.

"I have one heart," Fargo said, breaking in in Hopi. The other men muttered when they heard him speak their language. "I came from the north because the man called Hank Giffin sent a message that he needed help. So I came to the white man's pueblo on the hill to find him. But he was dead. Killed the same way . . ."

"That white man was marked by the *kachina* people!" a Hopi muttered in the back of the room. "The *kachina* tell even the white men that Hopis must go!" The others talked agitatedly among themselves until the old man raised his hand.

"Open the top of your heads!" the old man said. "Listen to me, Fire Dawn. Today Green Corn Standing, a brave warrior, has been killed. But still I do not believe *kachina* spirits kill Hopi. And they do not kill white men."

"And I say the spirits tell us what we must do!" Fire Dawn responded again, jumping to his feet. "Bear Paw is old and tired. He does not want to listen! Already we have lost eight of our braves. Including my father. Must everyone on the mesa die before we understand?"

"Hopi live here in *Túwanasaui*," the old man called Bear Paw said quietly but insistently. "It is the center of the universe, the center of the four directions and the four wanderings. Hopis live here. Hopis *stay* here."

"Then all Hopis will die!" said Fire Dawn again, his voice angry. "I say we must listen to the *kachina* people! I say we must go to the Red City!" The brave crossed to the ladder angrily and quickly ascended. He was followed by most of the rest of the men. Bear Paw shook his head sadly and looked around at the few remaining men. Fargo waited until the angry braves had gone before speaking again.

"When did the killings start?" Fargo asked.

"One moon ago," said Sun-Sky. The old man, Bear Paw, listened and was silent.

"And what is this about leaving the mesa?" asked Fargo.

"The *kachina* writings," Sun-Sky said. "The triangle means *Palátkwapi*—the Red City of the south. The sacred river runs underneath. And the small marks—"

"Like footprints?"

"Yes. They mean that we must leave this place and go to the Red City."

Fargo thought about this for a while. "Hank Giffin and Green Corn Standing were both killed by a blow to the head," Fargo said. "Did the others die this way?"

Sun-Sky nodded slowly before he spoke. "Yes, the tops of their heads were opened."

"What does that mean?" Fargo said. "You used that phrase before," he said to Bear Paw.

"It means *know this*," the old man explained. "Open the top of your head means to *learn*, to *know*. So Fire Dawn thinks the *kachina* spirits say that we should know to leave this place and go south. But I think the *kachina* people do not speak this way. They do not kill. I think we must open our heads to find the truth."

Bear Paw got slowly to his feet and climbed the ladder. Sun-Sky rose and Fargo followed him out of the *kiva*. Outside, the dark clouds had blown to the east and the golden light of late afternoon poured down on the adobe walls of the pueblo. Bear Paw stood blinking in the sun. He reached inside his buckskin shirt and brought out a small leather pouch from which he took a clear crystal rock that glittered in the sunlight. Bear Paw held the crystal up toward the sun and chanted in a low voice. Fargo glanced at Sun-Sky quizzically.

"My father is a great medicine man," the brave explained. "He has the power of sight. With his invisible eye, he can see many hidden things."

After a few minutes, Bear Paw returned the crystal to his pouch and turned toward Fargo. His leathery face was all smiles. "You are truly a one-hearted man," the old man said. "Come to stay in my dwelling for the night."

Fargo hesitated for a moment. His thoughts went back to the town of Mirage, to Arabella, her father and sister. They would be expecting him back at nightfall. And they would be hoping he had found the thief, Frederico. But all he had was a certainty that Zeb Connelly and the men of the Circle C had something to hide about seeing Frederico. Fargo knew he had to get back to Mirage.

Just then, he heard a shout. The young boy Fargo had seen earlier appeared and ran toward them. He was carrying something large and heavy in his arms. As he drew closer, Fargo saw it was a stone.

"Another *kachina* message," Sun-Sky said, despair in his voice. "For two moons, we have found the same message on many rocks around the mesa."

The boy's excitement had attracted the attention of

the other braves and they came running, drawing together in a circle as the boy approached Bear Paw.

"I found the *kachina* rock down by the water place!" the boy said, puffing from his run up the steep path to the top of the mesa. The boy deposited the flat sandstone slab at the old man's feet, then backed away. A gasp went around the circle as the Hopis read what was inscribed on the rock. Fargo saw a stick figure that seemed to be running above the image of a cloud. To one side, a sliver of moon was drawn above three slash marks.

"So!" Fire Dawn said triumphantly. "The *kachinas* have spoken! Tomorrow we will see with our eyes that *kachinas* speak the truth!" He stalked away toward the pueblo, while the other men gathered in small groups, talking anxiously. The old man stood alone and stared at the rock.

"I do not understand," Bear Paw said softly, his leathery face puckered with thought. "My eye did not see this thing. Maybe Fire Dawn is right. I am an old man. Maybe the *kachina* power is gone from me." He turned and walked away toward the pueblo.

"What has happened? What does it mean?" Fargo quietly asked Sun-Sky, who remained behind, looking at the rock.

"The picture says the *kachina* spirit will walk in the sky," the brave said, "at the time of three lights—that means dawn—on the new-moon day. That is tomorrow morning."

Fargo thought over the strange message as he glanced at the lowering sun. He could ride back to Mirage now and get there after dark. But he knew he'd turn around and come back to the mesa to see what happened the following morning. A *kachina* spirit walking in the sky? He doubted it. But someone had sent that message. And whoever was killing the Hopis, as well as Hank Giffin, was trying to get the Hopis to leave the mesa. This latest message was just another part of the plan. Fargo's thoughts immediately turned to Zeb Connelly, the Circle C, and the Hopi ranch hand, Running Dog. They had to be mixed up in this.

"I met one of your tribe up at the sheep ranch in the hills," Fargo said. "A man named Running Dog."

"He is not of our tribe," Sun-Sky said angrily, with a grimace. "Running Dog was born of the Spider clan." When Fargo looked puzzled, Sun-Sky explained. "All in the Spider clan are *núkpana*—evil! In ancient days, they helped Spider Woman melt the great ice of the north. And so they were banished. And then they tried to stop the running of the sacred river in the Red City." Sun-Sky made a quick circular gesture with his hand in the air as if warding off an evil spirit. "All Spider clan is *núkpana*. But come, let's not talk of that. Let us go to my father's house to eat. You are welcome in our dwelling."

In the ruddy light of sunset, Sun-Sky turned away and Fargo followed as he reviewed the brave's words in his mind. The fact that the Spider clan was considered evil explained why Running Dog had seemed so twisted and nasty when Fargo met him at the ranch. Running Dog had been banished by his people, not because of his own actions, but because he happened to have been born into the wrong family. So all his life Running Dog had been an outcast, belonging nowhere. A man like that could easily become a tool in the hands of someone else, Fargo thought. Someone like Zeb Connelly.

They paused as they crossed the main plaza. In the center was a low rock cairn. On it was a blanket-wrapped bundle. Fargo knew it was the body of Green Corn Standing. Several men and women stood nearby and a low keening drifted through the air. Beyond them, on the far side of the square, Fargo saw the tall, slender form of the widow named Raindrop.

The woman bent gracefully over a smoking, bee-hive-shaped oven and her long hair swept the ground. He watched as she removed the rocks from the opening and used a long wooden paddle to lift fresh bread from the coals inside. After she placed the bread into a basket, she turned to leave and noticed Fargo standing there. She lifted the basket of bread toward him with a smile, as if offering it to him, and stood brazenly returning his stare until Sun-Sky noticed the direction of Fargo's gaze.

"Raindrop pleases you?" Sun-Sky asked suddenly.

"She is very beautiful," Fargo said. "And not at all shy."

Across the plaza, Raindrop lowered the basket slowly and disappeared inside the pueblo. Sun-Sky laughed and pulled Fargo's arm. They arrived at Bear Paw's dwelling and entered the small, blanket-hung door.

Inside, the room was lit by oil-dish lamps placed in niches in the adobe wall. In one corner a fragrant mesquite fire blazed, the smoke rising through a hole in the ceiling. The old man sat on a deep ledge, which ran the circumference of the room and functioned as both seat and table. Bear Paw motioned for them to sit. Fargo rested against the cool adobe, feeling no need to speak. He felt himself relax for the first time all that long day. Hunger clawed at him. In a few minutes, the blanket was pushed back and several women entered, carrying pottery jars and baskets full of steaming, fragrant stews and dried fruits. They placed these on the ledge and quietly exited. Then Raindrop entered with the basket of warm bread. As she put it down beside Fargo, she hesitated and then spoke.

"You are the one they call the Wanderer," Raindrop said softly. "You are a warrior with many stories." She had wide cheekbones, a long, arching neck, glistening hair, and large, dark eyes.

"I am Skye," he said with a smile.

She repeated his name several times, as if tasting the word, and then left the room with a smiling backward glance. Bear Paw cleared his throat and passed a basket of piñon nuts to Fargo. They ate in silence for a while, feasting on the *knukquivi*, a delicious stew of lamb and corn, until Fargo felt the edge of hunger leave him. After a time, one of the women returned and gathered the baskets and earthenware.

Bear Paw rose, retrieved a deerskin parfleche which hung from a peg on the wall, and pulled out a long reed pipe. He stuffed the pipe with a pungent herb, lit it, and handed it to Fargo. The sweetish smoke burned his throat, and Fargo felt the rush of the herb's power pass through him. He passed the pipe back to the old man. Time seemed to slow, and Fargo's thoughts drifted like clouds—to the town of Mirage, to Arabella, to the terrible sight of Hank Giffin's mutilated body in the dark shack. If only he'd arrived before Giffin had been killed. What had Giffin found out that made him telegraph for help? Fargo recalled what Eben Blackwell had said about Hank Giffin, about how he'd spent a lot of time with the Indians and seemed to get along with them.

After a long, drifting time, Fargo spoke. "Did you know Hank Giffin?" he said, interrupting the silence. The smoke hung heavy and fragrant in the air. Sun-Sky exhaled a cloud and passed the pipe back to Fargo.

"Giffin was my friend. A friend of the Hopi. Even if he was *kachada*," Bear Paw said quietly, using the Hopi word for white man. "Years ago, when he first came to the center of the universe, he rode on his horse into Hopi land. But he was not like most white men. He did not try to ride up the mesa uninvited. Every day for many moons he camped at the ghost place."

"The ghost place?" Fargo interrupted. "Where's that?"

"That white-man pueblo down near the water," Sun-Sky explained. Fargo remembered the deserted ranch he'd seen, with the abandoned shack and busted corrals.

"This white man was wise. He waited for friends to come to him," Bear Paw said. "Every morning at the time of three lights I stood at the edge of the mesa and I looked down to see him waiting. After the cold time came twice, I walked down to name him. I called him Waiting Man. And he became my friend. My brother."

Bear Paw was silent then and Fargo could tell that the old man was lost in remembering. Fargo thought back to his own memories of Hank Giffin, when he'd been Sergeant Giffin in an army camp in Kansas Territory. He had a vague memory of how Giffin had been interested in the Cheyenne tribe and how he'd been one of the few men in the U.S. Army who troubled to learn the Indian's language.

"Yesterday, I did not believe Fire Dawn," the old

man continued, "when he told me he had found the body of Waiting Man by the Red-Finger-Pointing. And that the *kachina* spirits wrote their message on Waiting Man, too. I thought Fire Dawn was too quick to believe these *kachina* messages. So, I hurried to Red-Finger-Pointing. But the white men had come and taken away the body of Waiting Man. So last night I went to see my old friend." The old man paused and stared into the fire as Fargo took in the meaning of the old man's words.

"You mean . . . *you* went to see Hank Giffin's body?" Fargo asked. He remembered the mysterious figure he'd seen the night before in Mirage, the light in the shack and the quiet footsteps of someone slipping away in the darkness, past the watchmen. He realized how much of an effort it must have been for the old man to have ridden over all that way and then crept into town to see Giffin's body. "And you left an eagle feather there, on Hank Giffin's chest."

Bear Paw's eyes were far away and he spoke as if in a dream. "Now Waiting Man can fly to the hunting ground. And his enemies cannot follow."

The old man got up very slowly and pulled the wool serape around his shoulders. The blanket at the front doorway fluttered as a chill desert wind reached into the room. Without another word, Bear Paw went out into the night.

"It is good to get a few hours of sleep," Sun-Sky said, standing and stretching. "Before the time of the three lights, we will be up to watch the coming of the *kachina*, who will walk in the sky."

"Do you believe that?" Fargo asked him.

Sun-Sky's brow darkened. "I do not know," he said. "*Kachina* spirits have great power. But I have never heard of them killing innocent people in this way. But who can explain the ways of the *kachinas*? Maybe they are angry."

"I think somebody is trying to drive you out of this land," Fargo said. "And I think Running Dog may be mixed up in it."

"No. That cannot be. Running Dog is banished," Sun-Sky said. "If he comes back to the mesa land, his two hearts will stop beating and he will die. He would not come back here."

"Maybe he doesn't believe that," Fargo said.

Sun-Sky chewed over these words for a few minutes. "There is much to think about," he said as he turned to leave. "This will be your place for tonight. And I will wake you before the time of the three lights."

After Sun-Sky left, Fargo spread several of the thick woven blankets on the ledge to make a soft bed and extinguished the oil-dish lamps. The fire had died down and he added a couple of mesquite sticks from a pile by the door. Then he undressed, stowing his boots and shirt and Levi's on the ledge nearby. He positioned his Colt beside the folded blanket that would be his pillow. As always, the Arkansas toothpick was strapped to his ankle.

Fargo slipped between the rough wool blankets and his thoughts turned to the people he'd left behind in Mirage. He hoped Arabella and her father were not unduly worried that he hadn't returned by nightfall, as he'd promised. He was just mulling over the strange *kachina* messages when he heard soft footsteps approaching from outside. Fargo, his eyes on the doorway, put his hand on the butt of his Colt. He relaxed as the blanket moved and Raindrop stepped inside the warm room.

She had changed her clothes and was wearing a white doeskin dress fantastically decorated with bead-work, silver squash blossoms, porcupine quills, bear claws, and seashells on thongs that swayed prettily with her every movement. Her long dark hair cascaded over her shoulders and her dark eyes looked at him questioningly. Fargo smiled in answer.

"You look very beautiful," he said. He suspected that the highly ornamented garment had been her wedding dress. She dimpled at the compliment and walked forward a step into the firelight. She stood as if waiting. Fargo sat up and the blankets fell away from him. Her gaze rested on his powerful chest and muscular arms and then returned to his face. "But you must wait another moon, mourning Black Crow," Fargo said. "And I am not a marrying man."

"I understand. You are the Wanderer," Raindrop said. "So a woman such as I can . . ." She did not know what to say next so she waved her hand helplessly in the air. "After the winter, the first-green-plant moon must come again." Fargo realized she was talking about spring and about her own loneliness during the time of mourning her dead husband and about the stirring of desire. He felt that too as he looked at her in the firelight. He slowly stood and the blankets fell away from him. Raindrop's eyes dropped to his shorts and he knew she could see, beneath the fabric, the wantingness swollen and hard between his legs.

With one fluid motion, like wind across a field of grass, Raindrop pulled the white deerskin dress off over her head and stood proudly before him. Her body was magnificent, long and lean, supple and strong. Her legs, like those of a doe, were brown and slender.

And her small breasts, high and round, were two generous moons. The dark triangle glistened in the firelight.

Fargo stripped off his shorts and his manhood stood ready, wanting her, wanting to be inside. He moved across the room toward her and took her in his arms. She pressed her warm, silken flesh against him with a low purr, her eyes half-closed with pleasure as he stroked her back and bent to kiss her. His lips found hers and she opened to him, taking his tongue into her sweet mouth as her hands sought and found him.

He stood for a time, pressed against her warm nakedness, his mouth on hers, hands gently exploring her long curves. Then a gust of cold night wind fluttered the door covering and Fargo felt her shiver. He pulled her toward the nest of blankets. Raindrop lay down and Fargo stretched out beside her, kissing her gently here and there. She smelled of sweet sage. He took a hard nipple between his lips as his hand found its way across her tight belly and to the warm nap. She was ready for him and her legs came up as he turned and slowly slipped inside her.

"Oh, yes," she murmured. "The Wanderer has come and brought the first-green-plant moon. Ah, ah."

Fargo moved slowly in her wet sheath, back and forth, stroking her first one way and then the other. He paused and slipped his hand between them to find the folded tightness and teased it gently.

"Oh, oh!" she said, shuddering beneath him. He rubbed her faster and felt her hips bucking and grinding beneath him. She cupped her own breasts and held them up toward him as if offering herself to him as she cried out. He felt the force gathering in her and he took his hand away, lifting her hips and pushing into

her, feeling himself engorged against the firm small-
ness of her. He could feel it beginning, the urgent
gathering of exquisite pleasure, the unstoppable coming as he plunged into her faster and faster now, unable to slow or to stop.

Raindrop tensed beneath him and then let out a sob,
shuddering again and again just at the moment that
Fargo felt the explosion, the incredible release into
her again and again and again, until he felt at one with
her, having given her everything, and then he slowed
and stopped.

"Oh," Raindrop sighed. She wrapped her strong
arms around him and pulled him down on top of her.
He felt the waves of sleep rising as she nestled into
him. He heard the mesquite embers pop once, and
then he let himself float away into darkness.

Fargo came awake and felt the woman curled up inside the curve of his body as he lay on his side. He
knew several hours had passed. The fire was out.
There was no light at the small window opening, but
dawn was not too far off. And he wanted to scout all
around the mesa top well before the light came. He
slowly inhaled the warm sage fragrance of her neck,
reluctantly slipped his hand from between the soft pil-
lows of her breasts, and quietly eased out from under
the blankets. Despite his efforts to not disturb her
sleep, Raindrop awoke. She turned over and groped
for him, catching his hand. He felt her hold it to her
cheek for a brief instant, as if she didn't want to let
him go.

"Is it the time of three lights already?" she asked.

"Soon," Fargo said.

"No," she said. "It is still the middle of the night.

The sun will not come for many hours." He smiled into the darkness. They both knew she was wrong about that.

"I wish that, too," Fargo said, bending over to kiss her fragrant hair and slipping his hand out of hers. "Maybe there'll be another night for us. Before one of the men in your tribe gets you to marry him," he added playfully, reaching over to tickle her ribs.

He heard her giggle in the darkness. Fargo rose and located his buckskin jacket, pulled matches from his pocket, and lit one of the oil-dish lamps in a niche. He turned and saw Raindrop arise from the blankets, her lean golden body shining in the dim light. She smiled at his glance. For a moment he considered staying with her another hour, but he had to be outside keeping an eye on the mesa. He unwillingly donned his clothes as she slipped into the decorated deerskin dress. As he pulled on his boots, she gave him a quick, warm kiss and left silently.

The cold desert wind blew steadily from the west as Fargo made his way through the starlit streets of the sleeping pueblo. Several braves were keeping watch and they hailed him as he walked by. Once he had passed the border of the small settlement, he made his way across the naked rock and tufted grass of the mesa top. His eyes gradually adjusted to the darkness, but he kept a lookout for the shallow depressions in the rock in which the Hopis trapped rainwater.

The edge of the mesa yawned before him and he stopped, looking westward across the vast desert land that lay below him. In the pale starlight, he could barely make out the black shape of the deserted ranch below. Across the empty miles, in the arms of the dark hills, lay the town of Mirage. His thoughts flitted briefly over Arabella and then turned to wondering what would happen when the dawn arrived.

The message of the sandstone slab had indicated that a *kachina* spirit would appear in the sky. It was incredible, thought Fargo. He suspected it was some kind of a trick being pulled off by whoever was leaving those damn messages. Some kind of show put on to scare the Hopis off their land once and for all. But from what he'd heard the day before in the *kiva*, Fire Dawn and most of the Hopi men really did believe that the *kachinas* were telling the tribe to leave their land and go south. And if a *kachina* really did appear in the sky . . .

Fargo took another look over the dark land. A slight movement caught his eye—something small moving on the pale streak of a sand wash a mile or so away. He stared at the place until spots of light danced before his eyes, but he saw nothing else. Coyote, he thought. No, too small. Maybe some wild horses grazing in the night. He watched for another hour, eyes scanning the silent sagebrush, tumbled rock, and salt flats, but he saw nothing else. The eastern horizon began to show a pale light. Fargo headed back to the pueblo.

The whole tribe had awakened early in anticipation of the appearance of the *kachina* spirit. They had gathered in the main plaza. The sandstone slab with the picture message had been placed on a large stone altar. In the half-light of predawn, Fargo could see that everyone had donned festival clothing. Among a crowd of women, he spotted Raindrop in the white deerskin dress she had worn for him the night before. She was also wearing a large, flat, painted headpiece, as were most of the women. Bear Paw stood silently in the center of the plaza in a fancy beaded tunic. In one hand the medicine man held a bundle of eagle feathers and in the other a prayer stick. Even the children were wearing colorfully decorated skins and woven shirts. Fargo felt a hand on his arm and turned to see Sun-Sky in a yellow leather shirt sewn with seashells and quills.

"Are there guards around the village?" Fargo asked.

"Yes. And at the top of the path to the lowland," Sun-Sky answered. Fargo heard the quiver of excitement in Sun-Sky's voice, even though he knew the young brave did not believe the messages were really from the spiritual world. "Do you think . . . what do you think will happen?"

"I have no idea," Fargo said frankly.

The eastern sky continued to brighten moment by moment, and small tufts of molten gold clouds dotted the horizon. The Indians gradually grew quieter as they waited for the coming of the dawn—the time of the three lights. Red Dawn and several other impatient braves paced back and forth, their faces turned to the clear sky above. Bear Paw stood silent, head bowed, in the center. The nervous suspense was so thick in the air that several of the children had started to cry and were being comforted by their mothers.

Fargo broke away and walked out of the pueblo to check on the braves who were keeping watch on the only path up the mesa. It had occurred to him several times that perhaps the intent of the message had been to make the tribe vulnerable to attack. The brave guarding the path was a young man named Hungry Eye because of his excellent sight. He assured Fargo that from his vantage point he had seen nothing. No one was coming up the path.

Fargo was just heading back to the plaza when the first golden rays of sun struck his eyes. He stopped short and glanced up into the clean air and saw . . .

"Goddamn nothing," he exclaimed under his breath. He hurried forward again, glancing at the sky from time to time. When he reached the plaza, he found that all the Hopis were standing in silence, their faces to the sky as they waited for the promised manifestation. The sun slipped upward by degrees and at last hung free of the horizon. And still there was nothing to see.

An hour later, when the sun had burned from gold to white and the heat of the day was beginning to be felt, Bear Paw finally signaled that the vigil was ended. The time of the three lights had passed and no *kachina* had appeared. The women took their children away into the buildings and the young boys were sent off to fetch the day's supply of water from the stream below. Some of the men wandered off. For the next half hour, a small group of braves, including Fire Dawn, gathered around Bear Paw and the sandstone slab. They stood reading the pictures again and again and talking quietly. Fargo, who could catch most of the words, knew they were asking themselves if they had misinterpreted the message. Fargo left them to their puzzling and was just heading back to check on the guards when a shrill scream pierced the air.

Fargo ran toward the sound, which came from the direction of the mesa pathway. The young boy who had cared for the Ovaro the day before came running up the path and shot past the guard. The boy was running as if he had seen a ghost. Fargo ran after the kid—nothing but an antelope could run as fast as a young Indian. What the hell was going on? Shouts came from the plaza as the group of men ran forward to meet the boy. When Fargo ran up, the kid was babbling, talking a mile a minute and gesticulating wildly as the men gathered around him. Women and children, drawn by the excitement, ran toward them in a huge crowd.

"The . . . *kachina* spirit is . . . like a cloud!" the kid was saying, between gasps of air. "Down at the . . . water place. You can see!"

A shout went up from the Hopis and like a stampeding herd they rushed toward the path, which descended the mesa to the stream below and the deserted ranch. Fargo was swept along in the crowd of shouting Indians, who were running hell-bent down the side of the mountain. There was no way to stop himself or anyone else, Fargo thought. The excitement had carried them all away. Fargo realized they were in trouble. Most of the Hopis were unarmed. And all the women and children were with them. Their horses had been left behind at the pueblo. He felt his stomach knot with dread. Was this the plan? Lure the entire unarmed tribe off the top of the mesa and then massacre them?

"Wait! Wait!" he called out to the braves running near him. "This might be an ambush!"

But he might have been yelling at the wind for all the notice they took of him. He stepped aside and let others pass as he looked up the steep descent and considered fighting his way back to the top to get his pinto. But, he realized, with the crowd descending it would take forever. He peered down the trail, looking for Sun-Sky or Bear Paw. Maybe they could help him reason with the tribe, try to stop them from rushing into danger. But they were nowhere to be seen. Fargo swore and shouted desperately again at the Indians near him. But they ignored him and plunged down the steep switchbacks.

Fargo realized it was hopeless. At least he had his Colt. And the throwing knife strapped to his ankle. Goddamn. One gun, a few bullets, a blade. He doubted he could save the tribe if they met up with trouble at the bottom of the mesa. He turned and rejoined the descent. But with every step, Fargo felt more sure they were running straight into disaster.

In ten minutes, Fargo reached the desert floor. The crowd of Hopis surged along, heading for the creek and the promised miracle. He scanned the terrain around them. On this side of the mesa, facing the hills and the town of Mirage, the land was flat. But there was a lot of sagebrush out there. Enough to hide a whole army of attackers. Ahead, he saw the creek and the deserted ranch. Beyond them, the base of the mesa was littered with tumbled boulders, which grew thicker and thicker around the south side of the huge butte. Fargo hurried up to the crowd standing by the creek. He spotted the boy, who pointed excitedly toward the southern end of the mesa rock face.

Fargo stared, blinked, and stared again. He wanted to pinch himself, but he knew he was seeing what he thought he was seeing.

There, halfway up the sheer rock face, was a large ledge that protruded outward, silhouetted against the bright sky beyond. And floating two yards above the ledge, hanging suspended in the sky, was a man—or something—with a huge black-and-white face, extravagant feathers, and a gigantic chest striped black and white. The *kachina* spirit raised its hands and began to dance in the sky. Around him, the Hopi stood awestruck, silent and openmouthed as they watched the amazing sight.

Fargo tightened his grip on the butt of his Colt. If an attack was going to come, it would come right about now.

5

Fargo glanced around at the sagebrush, expecting to see the rush of an attack. His hand was firm on the butt of his Colt. But all was still. He glanced up again at the strange sight of the huge *kachina* figure hanging in the clear sky, dancing and lifting its arms upward in slow circling motions. All around him, the Hopis stood in silent amazement. He spotted Sun-Sky and moved forward to stand beside him. The young brave seemed transfixed by the miraculous sight.

After a few minutes, the *kachina* raised its arms to the sky and then seemed to leap upward. As it fell toward the ledge, its body disappeared, feet first, in a sudden flash of light and smoke, as if the sky had swallowed it. There was a long silence as the Hopis continued to watch expectantly up toward the rock ledge, but all that could be seen now was empty sky above the silhouette of the rock ledge. Fargo looked around again. Still no attack.

"You see?" Fire Dawn said, breaking the silence. "I was right. The *kachina* spirit has shown itself. We must go tomorrow at first light! Get everything ready for the journey. We must leave this place and go to the Red City!"

"To the Red City!" Others took up the cry and the

tribe turned and hurried back toward the path to the mesa. Only Bear Paw and Sun-Sky remained behind. The old man removed the seeing crystal from his leather pouch and lifted it toward the sky, staring through it intently. Fargo continued to watch the rock ledge above. What the hell had gone on up there?

Then he saw it. For an instant, the patch of sky above the jutting rock seemed to bend inward and he saw a piercing flash of light and then a moving figure—a man's figure. But in a moment it was gone and the sky was empty again.

"Did you see that?" Fargo asked Sun-Sky.

"What was it?" the brave asked, puzzled.

"Some kind of trick," Fargo said. "How can we get up to that ledge?"

"There are two ways," Sun-Sky said. "But we must go around the mesa toward those big rocks." The brave pointed southward, past the deserted ranch, where the gigantic tumbled boulders littered the land at the base of the huge butte. Fargo saw that it was a long way to walk—or to run. For an instant, he considered returning to the mesa top to bring the pinto, but then he realized that the trip would take too long. Whoever had been up on that rock ledge would be long gone. Their only hope was to get up there fast and try to catch him. Or them.

"It was not *kachina*," Bear Paw said wonderingly as he lowered his crystal and held it clasped in his palm. "But it was *kachada*—a white man. I saw his face." Fargo thought of Zeb Connelly and he described him. "No," Bear Paw said slowly. "I have seen the big sheep man and it was a different face."

Fargo felt the moments slipping away. There was

no time to talk now. Every second gave whoever was up on that ledge time to get away.

"Let's get up there," Fargo said to Sun-Sky. He turned and followed the young brave, who set off at a swift loping run. Fargo was surprised when Bear Paw trailed them as well. The wiry old man kept up pretty well. They ran past the deserted ranch and then hit the rugged terrain to the south. It was hard going, running in the sucking sandy soil and dodging the huge red boulders, many as large as two-story houses. After a few more minutes, they came to a faint path that led up between boulders, climbing the twisted stone face of the mesa cliff. Sun-Sky had started climbing when Fargo called out to him. "You said there are two ways to get up there?" he asked.

The brave turned around. "Yes. The other path is further to the south and well hidden."

"Then I'll go this way," Fargo suggested. "You guard the other path in case they try to get away that direction. You armed?"

In answer, Sun-Sky pulled a long blade from a leather sheath at his waistband. "I will be careful," he said, his dark eyes blazing.

Bear Paw came striding up just as Fargo and Sun-Sky were parting. The old man took in the situation at once and indicated that he would follow behind Fargo. The path was a steep scramble, more like a climb. In some places, Fargo had to grab hold of the tough cliffrose bushes that dug their roots hard into the rocky soil. He kept his eyes ahead for trouble as the ledge loomed above him, but from his perspective it was impossible to see anything. An occasional sound of tumbling rock from below told him that the old man was not too far behind.

Finally, he spotted a steep ascent just ahead, bare rock just below the lip of the ledge into which a few hand- and foot-holds had been carved. Fargo glanced upward, listening intently. He heard nothing. No movement. If there was someone up there, Fargo would be a sitting duck, clinging to the naked rock. He signaled to Bear Paw, who was a hundred yards below, and then began the final ascent. Lifting himself inch by inch, using the hand- and toe-holds, Fargo tried not to make any sound. At last he reached the lip of the wide ledge. He eased himself upward by small degrees until he could see across the shelf. There was no one there.

Fargo swore inwardly and dragged himself over the top. He got to his feet and took a swift look around. The ledge, halfway up the mesa cliff, had a commanding view of the broken land below. A few dozen yards away, on the far south end, he saw the other path that led downward. They must have escaped that way. Sun-Sky was waiting at the bottom of that trail. There was no time to lose.

Fargo quickly examined the ground and saw fresh footprints in the dust. Three or four men in boots. And then some strange prints that he could not identify—a couple of wheel tracks too small for a wagon. And then two long, narrow indentations in the dust in a wide V, its point toward the valley below. Fargo hesitated for just a moment, looking at the odd tracks. Then he realized he needed to get down to where Sun-Sky was waiting. There was no time to wait for Bear Paw. The old man would follow at his own pace.

Fargo started to descend the southern path. This trail was much gentler than the one he had ascended. It wound back into a steep coulee, switchbacked and descended slowly between huge rocks. The boot prints and wheel tracks were fresh in the feathery dust. He tried to keep an eye out on the view below, but it was often impossible to see because of the big boulders in the way.

The trail had almost reached the bottom of the mesa when Fargo heard gunfire. One shot, like a small pop, echoed among the rocks. He heard the whine of the bullet ricocheting, followed by a second shot. He immediately drew his Colt and ran forward. Because of the echoing rocks, it was impossible to tell exactly which direction the shots had come from. But Fargo knew he had only to follow the tracks.

The trail was almost flat now, winding between the huge red boulders, many like small mountains. He had just rounded one of them when he heard the creak of saddle leather, horses snorting, and then several men's voices. Fargo dashed forward as the jangling of spurs and the beat of horses' hooves reached his ears. He came to a small, round clearing protected on all sides by towering rocks. The sound of the retreating horses was already dying away. They had escaped.

Goddamn, Fargo thought to himself. He would give anything to have his pinto with him just at that moment. He wondered where Sun-Sky had gone. Fargo gave a low whistle, like a burrowing owl. But he heard nothing in return. He began searching the rocks all around the clearing and suddenly spotted a moccasin protruding from a nearby rock. He hurried to the spot. Sun-Sky lay on the ground, his dark eyes staring at the sky above. In his hand was his knife, and the dark bullet hole dead center in his chest told the rest of the story.

Fargo swore as he stood over the body for a moment. He'd only known Sun-Sky for a day and yet he had known him to be a good man. He had been a levelheaded brave who someday would have taken his father's place as leader of the tribe. And now he was dead. Whoever had done this would pay for it, Fargo told himself silently. He was almost certain now that Zeb Connelly and the men of the Circle C were involved.

Fargo leaned over and closed Sun-Sky's eyes. Then he laid the body out, straightening the legs and crossing the arms over the chest. There was nothing more to be done but to wait for Bear Paw to catch up. Fargo took a seat on a rock in the shade.

The old man arrived a few minutes later. Fargo stood when he caught sight of him. Bear Paw's face was grave as he looked around the clearing for his son and did not see him. Fargo realized the old man had heard the shot, too, and probably had guessed what had happened. Fargo nodded toward the place where Sun-Sky's body lay.

The old man disappeared behind the rocks and stayed there for some time. The midmorning sun was pouring its heat down on the rocks. Finally, Bear Paw returned. He looked even older than before, his leathery face like a mask, his eyes hollow. Bear Paw sat down beside Fargo and after a few minutes he spoke. "The tracks on the ledge did not belong to a *kachina*. And there were other strange marks. I do not know what they were, but I know they were made by *kachada*. They are not Hopi."

"They are white men for sure," Fargo said. "I think it's Zeb Connelly trying to get your tribe to leave this land. The men in Mirage told me that in the winter the sheep graze on Hopi land, but that you don't mind."

Bear Paw's eyes narrowed as he considered Fargo's words. "The sheep men have given us meat. And sometimes wool. We have let them come sometimes to the edge of the Hopi lands. But the sheep have eaten all the yellow grass there. And we do not want white men's sheep everywhere. Two moons ago, we told the sheep men to find another place for the winter. Take the sheep to the north or south. But this is Hopi land."

So Connelly had lied, Fargo thought. The big rancher had said the Indians were satisfied with the arrangement he'd made. So when the Hopis said no, Connelly had come up with this diabolical plan to get the Hopis to leave. Yeah, Zeb Connelly struck him as just the kind of selfish bastard who would stop at nothing to guarantee himself more rangeland. And when the Hopis left, the Circle C sheep would have full run of the cool mountain meadows during the hot summers, as well as the warm, flat lowlands spotted with grass for the winter. Only one thing didn't make sense. Most of the Circle C sheep belonged to the men of Mirage. So was Connelly doing this for their benefit? Or were they in on it too? And what about Eben Blackwell, who had seemed so trustworthy? Fargo felt doubt assail him and knew he had to get back to town. And fast.

"I will return to the pueblo to get my horse," Fargo said. "And then I must go. Tell your people what you have seen. Sun-Sky was not killed by a *kachina* spirit."

Bear Paw nodded and walked off toward the body. Fargo followed. The old man suddenly stopped and put his hands beneath his son, and Fargo realized Bear

Paw intended to carry Sun-Sky back to the pueblo. Of course he did not want to leave the body here.

"Let me do that," Fargo said, pushing the old man aside gently. He hoisted Sun-Sky's body over his shoulder and they set off. It was a long way back, through the boulders around the mesa, past the ghost ranch and the creek, and finally ascending the path to the pueblo. But, preoccupied with thoughts of Zeb Connelly, Fargo hardly noticed the weight of Sun-Sky's body or the passing time.

It was almost noon when they topped the mesa. Two braves spotted them immediately and cried out in surprise and dismay. They ran forward and bore Sun-Sky's body toward the pueblo. Bear Paw spotted the boy who had been in charge of the horses and sent him to fetch the Ovaro, double-quick. And then the old man followed his son's corpse, walking slowly.

There was no time to stop here for rest or a meal, Fargo thought. He had to get back to Mirage and get some answers.

The pinto came galloping from the direction of the pueblo with the boy riding it. Fargo laughed and felt the tension drain from him. His Ovaro almost never let a stranger on its back unless Fargo was around. But the horse had obviously sensed the boy knew what he was doing. The Ovaro came to a halt and the boy slid down, his head hanging as if he expected to be punished for riding the horse.

"You ride well," Fargo said, tousling the boy's hair before he swung into the saddle. "The pinto likes you." The boy flashed a wide grin.

The Ovaro plunged down the trail. Its powerful chest muscles and sturdy legs sprang against the jarring impact of their fast descent. In a few minutes

Fargo had reached the flatland and was speeding past the creek, the ghost ranch, and out into the sage lands. He headed toward the western hills.

It was midafternoon by the time he galloped into Mirage. He pulled up in front of Eben Blackwell's sprawling shack and dismounted. He crossed the porch and paused, intending to beat the thick layer of trail dust off his clothing before he went inside. But the door flew open and Arabella ran out. She threw herself on him and gave him a big kiss.

"Skye! Skye!" she laughed. "We were all so worried about you! Where have you been?" She suddenly paused and sneezed, then backed away. The fine grit from his gallop across the plain dusted the front of her pink dress. She sneezed again and Fargo laughed. She laughed, too. Fargo removed his hat and beat it against his arms, chest, and thighs, throwing off a great cloud of yellow dirt.

"Mr. Fargo!" The little gray-haired magician hurried across the porch, his hand extended. "We were most concerned about you." He pumped Fargo's hand as if they'd never met before.

Adrienne appeared at the door, too, followed by Eben Blackwell, whose face lit up with relief. Adrienne's expression was unreadable, Fargo thought.

"I could use some grub," Fargo said. "I'll tell you where I've been. I've got some questions for you, Eben."

Blackwell nodded and bustled away. As soon as Fargo had unsaddled, watered, and fed the pinto, he returned to Blackwell's to find a couple of thick meat sandwiches and a cool beer on the big table. Everyone was waiting for him. While he ate, he told a short version of what he'd seen up at the Circle C. He watched

Eben's expression closely. Blackwell looked puzzled and thoughtful. Then Fargo told about his trip to the mesa, about the *kachina* message and the strange sight of the *kachina* spirit dancing in the air.

"Why . . . why, that's *my* trick! I *invented* that trick! It's my Wondrous Floating Woman!" Magnus exclaimed. His face reddened and he jumped to his feet and shook his fist. "Why . . . why, that means that little bastard thief, Frederico Connelly, is mixed up in this!" Fargo felt himself go cold at the name.

"Frederico . . . *Connelly*?" Fargo repeated.

"Sure," Magnus said, puzzled. "His name's Fred Connelly."

Eben Blackwell's eyes narrowed. "Like Zeb Connelly."

"Who's *that*?" Magnus asked suspiciously. Adrienne shifted uncomfortably in her chair. Fargo turned to look at her.

"Why don't you tell us what you know, Adrienne?" Fargo said. She flashed him an angry look and shook her head defiantly. Magnus strode to her side and stood over her.

"What do you know about this?" the magician hissed, anger boiling in his eyes. "You were always too good for that low-down, two-bit hustler. But you wouldn't listen to me. You felt sorry for him and you had to help him out." Magnus's voice rose hysterically. "Maybe you even helped him steal my wagon?" Magnus seized her arm and shook her violently.

Fargo pulled the little magician away from her. "Hold on now," he admonished Magnus. "I'm sure she didn't know Frederico was a thief."

Adrienne shot him a grateful look and the tears welled in her eyes. "I didn't know. Honest," she said, burying her face in her hands. Arabella moved toward her sister and stood protectively over her, one arm around her shoulders. "He . . . Fred always told me he was going to go to his uncle's ranch."

"His *uncle*," Blackwell whispered thoughtfully, nodding his head.

"I knew I'd heard of Mirage before," Arabella said. "I must have heard Fred mention it."

"You could have saved me a lot of trouble if you'd told me this earlier," Fargo shot at Adrienne. Her eyes filled with tears again.

"I'm sorry," she said. "I know it was wrong. But he promised he'd come back for me."

"And you believed him?" Fargo asked her.

Adrienne nodded her head.

"Do you still believe him?"

Adrienne dropped her eyes and shook her head no, then burst into sobs and ran from the room. Arabella followed. Eben Blackwell looked after them, his face a mixture of concern and relief.

"So this magician fellow you're trying to find is Zeb Connelly's nephew," Blackwell said after a moment, stroking his chin.

Fargo looked at him sharply. Just how much did Blackwell know about Zeb Connelly's plan to drive off the Indians? After all, his own sheep—and pocket—would benefit.

"I find it hard to believe that ole Zeb would get mixed up in something like this," Blackwell said defensively. "Why, we've all known Zeb for years and he's done a damn fine job tending our sheep up there. I've never known Zeb to be anything but straightforward." Blackwell tightened his mouth and looked pensively at Fargo. "No, I think Zeb's got a bad egg in his family. I bet he doesn't even know his nephew's around these parts. It's that nephew who's up to no good."

"But Fred Connelly arrived only a couple of days ago," Fargo pointed out. "And those killings have been going on for a month."

"You got a point there," Blackwell said. He thought for a moment. "I bet the nephew's in cahoots with that Indian fellow Zeb's got working up there."

"Running Dog," Fargo said. "I've thought of him. But what motive would he have for wanting the whole tribe to leave?"

Blackwell shrugged. "Who knows? Revenge or something, maybe. Those two are your culprits, Mr. Fargo," Blackwell said.

Fargo thought a moment about the fact that Running Dog was banished from the tribe. Revenge might be motive enough.

"Take my word," Blackwell continued. "Zeb Connelly is straight as an arrow. He's got nothing to do with this." Blackwell rose and stretched. "If it would settle your mind any, Mr. Fargo, I'll ask Zeb about it tonight. Everybody in town's going up to the ranch for the annual meeting. That's when Zeb reports on the profit and makes the payout." He turned to Magnus, who had sat listening in silence. "And you folks better get ready for the show."

"What show's that?" asked Fargo.

"Why, Zeb heard tell that we had a real magician in town," Blackwell said. "Asked if he'd come up and do a special show for everybody—all the ranch hands, too."

Right, Fargo thought. Frederico had heard that Magnus was hot on his tail. The invitation was just a trap to lure the old magician and his two daughters to the ranch. Hell, he didn't like the sound of this one bit. The same thought had obviously occurred to Magnus. He shot Fargo a look.

"You want to come along to see the show, Mr. Fargo?" Blackwell added magnanimously.

"I can't," Fargo lied. He saw Magnus's face fall. "I promised the Hopis I'd be back out there tonight to help them stand watch."

Blackwell shrugged and left for the stables to get the horses ready to leave. The front door slammed behind him.

"I am very worried about this Zeb Connelly," Magnus said.

"Zeb Connelly is a very dangerous man," Fargo said. "Despite what I said to Blackwell, I'll be coming along tonight. But I'll stay out of sight. And I suggest you leave your daughters here in town."

Fargo glanced up to see Arabella standing in the doorway.

"No," she said, having heard his words. "Where Papa goes, I go. And if it's dangerous, so what? That wagon of tricks is our livelihood. If we don't get it back, we're done for."

Fargo sat in thought for a long moment. There was no telling whether all the men of Mirage were in on the conspiracy with Zeb Connelly, or whether they were all being duped. Somehow he felt that Eben Blackwell was being misled by Connelly. But he couldn't be sure of it.

Fargo told them about the little Mexican cook, Juan, who had called to him and told him about seeing Frederico. But they'd been interrupted by Zeb before Juan could say more. And he told them also about the huge wooden barn near the big house. It had been padlocked. Fargo wondered if the painted wagon had been driven in there. It made sense.

"Listen," Fargo said at last, "I have a plan." He outlined it quickly, and Magnus added a few of his own ideas. Arabella had suggestions, too. Just when they had finished, a thought occurred to Fargo.

"What about Adrienne?" he asked. "Can she be trusted? After all, she'll be helping to bring Frederico to justice."

"I can be trusted," Adrienne's voice was heard saying. He turned to see her standing by the door. She had undoubtedly been there for some time and had heard the entire plan. "I'm sorry, Papa. And Arabella. And Mr. Fargo. I was wrong. Fred did deceive me, but I didn't want to admit it. I guess it was my pride."

Adrienne hung her head as Arabella jumped up to embrace her. Magnus was all smiles.

"I have my daughter back now," he said. "Now I know everything will go well. I wish I had the tricks in my wagon for tonight's show. But even without them, I promise you," Magnus said, waving his short arms dramatically in the air, "tonight I will give the performance of my life!"

The late afternoon sun spilled gold light across the hills as Fargo rode slowly through the piñons, on a slope overlooking the road leading to the Circle C. Below, between the pines, he glimpsed the men of Mirage, Magnus, and the two sisters riding behind. He decided to take a shortcut through the hills toward where the Circle C ranch lay. He turned the pinto away from the road and cantered up the hillside, careful to stay under the cover of the pines. For the next hour, he rode warily, hugging the edges of the meadows where the flocks of sheep grazed and slipping from one stand of trees to the next. Back in Mirage, he had ridden off ostensibly heading back to the Hopi mesa; but then he had doubled back and dogged the group leaving from town and heading to the ranch.

Fargo was riding through a stand of lodgepole pines. The last golden light of the sun filtered through the tall trunks. The ranch house would be coming up any minute now, he thought, as he heard the gurgle of a stream. The Ovaro heard it, too, smelled the water, and its ears stood up. Fargo knew that signal. He gave the horse a loose rein and let it wander toward the water. Fargo slid down as the pinto drank gratefully. He doffed his hat and leaned over to scoop up some clear water for himself. Suddenly, the Ovaro lifted its head and snorted. Fargo's Colt was out of its holster in a flash, but even that was too late.

"Drop it, mister," a voice said from behind him. Fargo tensed and was about to turn and fire when another voice spoke from off to his left.

"Do what he says. Drop it." In the silence, the click of a hammer being cocked punctuated the demand. From his right, Fargo heard another sound, the faint scrape of someone against the rough bark of a tree trunk. So there were three of them. And they had him surrounded and covered. Even if he managed to shoot one of them, they'd get him. He straightened up and slid the Colt back into its holster.

"On the ground," the first voice said insistently. "And kick it." Fargo did what he was told, but didn't kick it very far.

One of the men stepped out from behind a tree, a tough-looking sandy with muscles that looked like they'd been carved of stone. His pistol was aimed at a point right between Fargo's eyes.

Stupid, Fargo thought. Aim at a man's belly. That way if he moved you could adjust only slightly and still hit him. Aim at a man's head, and if he ducked, you'd never hit him in a million years. He hoped the other two were just as incompetent.

"Hi, there," Fargo said, trying to sound friendly. He kept his hands in the air. The man's ruddy face and blond hair didn't look familiar. Fargo was pretty sure he hadn't run into him the day before at the ranch. It was possible he could talk his way out. "No need to get excited. I'm just passing through," Fargo said, adopting an affable tone. "I stopped for a drink. No harm meant." The sandy relaxed slightly, but only slightly.

"You're trespassing, mister," he said.

"Really?" Fargo said, pretending surprise. "Sorry! I had no idea anybody lived up here. Just tell me which way to go and I'll get off your property. I'm heading over to the Piñon Trail." The big man moved forward and stooped to retrieve Fargo's Colt, then holstered his own.

"He's okay," he called out to the other two. They stepped from their hiding places, and Fargo knew instantly that he was in trouble. One of the men was the skinny guy named Bill. Bill did a double take at Fargo and recognition flashed across his face.

"Hey!" he said, raising the barrel of his gun. "I've seen this guy. He's a troublemaking bastard."

Fargo reacted instantly, diving toward the big sandy, who had his Colt in hand. At the moment he hit the big blond fellow, Bill pulled the trigger and a shot whizzed through the space where Fargo had been a second before. Fargo rolled over and over with the big man as they grappled for the Colt.

The blond's muscles were like solid rock and his meaty grip on the butt of Fargo's pistol was impossible to pry loose. Fargo was aware of the two other men nearby, and he kept rolling with the big man so they couldn't get a clear shot at him. They rolled up against a big rock, with the blond on top, and Fargo saw his chance. Summoning all his strength, he jerked the man's heavy arm hard against the rock, smashing the fist holding his Colt with a bone-shattering jolt.

The blond yowled in pain and his grip loosened for a split second. Fargo wrenched his pistol free. He jammed his left elbow into the man's gut and heard the breath leave him. In the next instant, Fargo wrenched the man's head toward the rock as well. His skull hit hard and the man fell heavily forward onto Fargo.

A rough hand seized Fargo's collar and pulled him upward. Bill, his long face flushed with fury, bent over him. Fargo stared down the long barrel of Bill's pistol. In a flash, Fargo reached up with one hand and deflected the barrel. Bill's gun roared and the bullet whined, ricocheting off a rock. With the other hand, Fargo pulled up his Colt and blasted the skinny man dead center. Bill, astonishment on his face, staggered backward holding his belly, dropped to his knees, and fell forward facedown. He didn't move again.

Fargo glanced around for the third man, who he had barely glimpsed before. He heard the jangle of spurs and the sound of hoofbeats. Goddamnit. His thoughts came in a flash. If the third man got away and alerted Zeb Connelly, the game was up. He'd have to catch him, and fast. By his own calculations, the ranch house had to be nearby. Fargo struggled out from under the body of the unconscious blond guy and sprinted toward his Ovaro. Swinging into the saddle, he took off, hell-bent, through the piney forest.

At his urging, the pinto, surefooted and swift, ran full-out through the woods, dodging tree trunks, missing them by bare inches. They followed the sound of the fleeing horseman. The rough bark scraped against Fargo's legs and the branches stung his face and his hands, but he didn't slow down. After a few minutes, he caught sight of the man, riding a spotted gray. For an instant, Fargo considered using his Colt, but then realized that he risked the gunfire being heard by Connelly's men. They galloped across a meadow and the Ovaro gained on the spotted gray.

The man turned around, sighted him, and pulled his gun. Fargo hunched down low in the saddle and the man hesitated for a moment, trying to get a bead on Fargo. Just then, the spotted gray entered the woods on the far side of the meadow and passed under a low-branched pine. The back of the man's head, caught by the branch, snapped hard and he left the saddle, tumbling to the ground. Fargo pulled up beside the man and dismounted. The man lay still, his neck broken. Fargo heard the pounding hooves of the horse as it ran on through the woods.

He'd have to stop the horse, too, he realized. If it wandered back to the ranch alone, they'd send out a party of ranch hands to look around. He mounted the pinto again and raced after the horse, but it was too late. Not far from where the man with the broken neck lay, the woods ended and a grassy valley stretched out below. Fargo paused in the cover of the woods and watched as the horse cantered down the hillside toward the maze of corrals and the group of log buildings that comprised the ranch. It slowed to a walk and then stopped and began grazing. Fargo whistled once, hoping the horse would wander back toward the woods, but it didn't take any notice. At some point, Fargo thought, someone would spot the saddled horse grazing in the meadow and would start asking questions. He hoped darkness came before anyone noticed.

The sound of approaching horses drew his attention and he watched as the men of Mirage came into view through the darkening twilight. Magnus and his two daughters rode in the center of the group, which halted and dismounted. Several men emerged from the bunkhouse and took their horses away to the corral next to the barn. Magnus, walking with his two daughters, paused for a moment and glanced around at the surrounding hills. Magnus knew he was out there. Fargo just hoped the magician wouldn't be too obvious about looking for him. After a moment, Arabella pulled on Magnus's arm and the group hurried inside. Now, if only their plan would work.

From the top of the hill and hidden in the edge of the wood, Fargo watched the big ranch house. He thought again about Eben Blackwell and the men of Mirage. If only he knew if he could trust them. Or were they in on this plan with Zeb Connelly?

He noticed a few ranch hands emerging from the various buildings. Then he saw more and more of them, until he counted nearly forty men. He expected to see them go inside the big house to see the magic show, but they didn't. Instead, they moved in small groups toward a corral at the far end, hidden from the house by a stand of cedar. What was going on? Blackwell had said that Zeb had invited Magnus and his

daughters to do a magic show for the ranch hands—
but they were riding out to go someplace.

The first bunch of ranch hands, rather than galloping away, led their horses at a walk all the way down
the road and out of sight. Obviously, they didn't want
to draw the attention of the men inside the ranch
house. They continued to leave in small groups, making no noise. Where the hell were they going? A half-
dozen stood talking by the barn. Something big was
up. Fargo wished he were close enough to hear what
was going on. He'd planned to wait until it was completely dark before venturing down. But after a moment's consideration, he decided to risk it.

He left the Ovaro untethered and sheltered in the
fringe of the dark pine wood. The faithful pinto never
wandered but would wait near where he left it until he
returned or whistled for it.

The blue dusk was deepening and the lights in the
ranch house winked golden as he left the trees and,
bent double, slipped down the hillside. There was no
cover to speak of, so he hoped the tall grass and the
dusk would hide him if someone happened to look in
his direction. He slowed down as he approached the
big barn and angled away so that the big wooden
building stood between him and the group of men
talking. He had just reached the barn and was edging
around one corner, where a huge pile of hay was
stacked against the wall, when he heard the front door
of the ranch house slam shut and Zeb Connelly's
voice. He edged closer to the corner to try to look
around it and realized the footsteps were coming
nearer and nearer.

"Come around this side, boys," Zeb was saying.
Fargo heard the jingle of keys as Connelly ap-

proached. Fargo dived into the hay, hastily piling it up to hide himself. He could just see out through the yellow straw. He saw Zeb Connelly's boots approaching. They stopped inches from Fargo's face.

The dust in the hay tickled his nose. Hell, if he sneezed, the jig was up. And he couldn't even move a finger without alerting them to his presence. He concentrated all of his effort into suppressing the sneeze. Meanwhile, he heard the voice of Zeb Connelly.

"Alright, boys," Zeb said. "You know the plan. First you burn out that stupid two-bit town of Mirage. And make it look like those Hopis did it. Then you come around and wait at the turnoff to the Piñon Trail. This meeting will break up around ten. They'll be riding back to town about eleven. You'll outnumber 'em two to one. Use every bullet you got. I don't want anybody to escape. Kill every goddamn one of 'em."

6

Fargo lay motionless in the straw, listening in disbelief to Zeb's diabolical plan to wipe out the men of Mirage.

"And make sure you stick the bodies with those Hopi lances we got from Running Dog," Zeb said. "We're gonna make it look just like those redskins burned and butchered the whole town and then ran away south. And afterward, nobody's going to ask any questions. We're gonna own that whole herd in the clear. And you boys will get a big cut. Now, get going."

So that was what Zeb had been planing all along, thought Fargo. With the Mirage men massacred and the Hopis tricked off their land, Zeb Connelly would gain control of the massive flock of mutton and a ranch almost as big as some of the states back East. And Zeb's plan could work, too. Everybody in Mirage had come to the ranch for the annual meeting, leaving behind only four men to guard the empty town. The watchmen would easily be overcome in a surprise attack by the ranch hands. And later, the rest of the men of Mirage were going to be ambushed and butchered on their way back to town. He'd have to warn them when they left the ranch house. But would they believe him?

He sat in thought for a moment and then realized that Zeb Connelly was playing right into their hands. After the magic show, Fargo would meet the magician as planned. Not only was his own scheme going to work, but it would be even easier than he'd expected. The only thing he hadn't counted on was the burning of Mirage. Most of the ranch hands were probably halfway there already. There was nothing he could do to stop the destruction of the town. But he could stop the ambush and the slaughter.

Through the straw, Fargo saw Zeb's boots move off and heard the jangle of Zeb's keys grow faint. Finally, he heard the slam of the ranch-house door and the distant crunch of gravel as Zeb's men walked toward the far corral. Fargo waited a minute, then poked his head out of the hay. No one was in sight and the wide meadow was nearly dark. The stars were out. Fargo pinched his nose a few times to keep the sneeze from coming. No telling who still might be standing on the other side of the barn.

He eased himself out of the pile of hay and slid along the wall, watching and listening. The clop of horses' hooves came to his ears. From the cover of the barn, he watched as six ranch hands moved down the road, leading their horses at a quiet walk. The occasional roar of laughter and applause drifted out from inside the big ranch house. Magnus and his daughters were performing the magic tricks they could do without the benefit of the gizmos in Magnus's wagon. Even though the men of Mirage had seen most of the tricks at Blackwell's already, they were an appreciative audience.

Fargo peered around at the big barn doors facing the ranch house. The padlock he remembered seeing on his previous visit was still in place. Now why would someone padlock a barn? He felt almost certain that Magnus's stolen wagon was inside. But where was Frederico? Zeb wasn't stupid. Undoubtedly he was just keeping Frederico out of sight. Fargo stared at the big ranch house and saw several lighted windows on the second story. That's probably where the bald-headed magician was cowering.

Fargo walked past the haystack to the side of the barn farthest from the big house. As he rounded the corner, he noticed a second pair of big doors. A small opening was cut in one of the doors. Fargo approached and examined the square hole. It was an old-fashioned door with an interior slide bolt and a hole just big enough for a man to get his arm inside to throw the bolt. Not that that mattered, because these doors were also padlocked on the outside.

Fargo looked into the dark, square hole, but he could make out nothing in the darker interior. He glanced about to make sure there was no one around and drew the matches from his jacket pocket. He struck one and, holding it between his fingers, put his hand in through the hole and lowered his head to peer through. In the dim light of the match's flame, Fargo could barely make out the big, square outline of Magnus's painted wagon. So, there it was. By the flickering light, he also saw that the floor inside the barn was covered with hay. Fargo extinguished the flame and brought the smoking match out, careful not to drop it inside. The barn was a virtual tinderbox. One spark on that dry hay and the whole barn would go up in a flash.

Fargo straightened up and moved around to the other side of the barn, which fronted the road. There was nothing to see there. All the ranch hands seemed to have left to incinerate the town of Mirage. He came around to the corner and peered at the ranch house again. He checked the windows that faced the barn and decided to make a dash for it. Bending low and on silent feet, he sped across the open yard and flattened himself against the log wall. He waited to make sure no one had spotted him.

After a few moments, Fargo eased his way along the side of the house until he reached a window. He slowly edged up to it, grateful to see it had wooden shutters on the inside, which would make it harder for anyone glancing at it to see his face looking in. The shutters were half-open, and between the slats he could see into the big room. The window was raised an inch and he could easily hear what was going on inside.

Magnus the Magnificent stood on a chair positioned in front of the huge stone fireplace. The men of Mirage sat in rows of chairs, facing him. Fargo had a perfect view right up the center aisle. Magnus tossed large silver rings into the air, which, as they descended, caught onto other rings, all of which looked as if they were solid. Magnus, keeping up a continuous patter of mumbo jumbo, occasionally whirled his cape, while Arabella passed him more rings and Adrienne held up the long and growing chain of interlocked rings. When the chain of rings reached all the way across the room, Adrienne and Arabella deftly folded the rings together and Magnus waved his hands, muttering some magic. They threw the rings into the air and they fell clanging to the floor, all separated again. The audience stomped and whistled. Magnus held up his hands for quiet.

"And now, the lovely Arabella will perform the most daring and impossible feat of humankind," Magnus announced. "She will discover what is in the thoughts of another. Yes, my friends, she will read the human mind!" Fargo leaned forward in anticipation.

Swirling his cape grandly around him, the little magician hopped down from the chair and advanced through the audience. Meanwhile, Adrienne helped Arabella onto the chair and draped a blue satin robe covered with stars around her shoulders. Fargo smiled to himself. Even without all their equipment, the three managed to put on a real show. Magnus looked at the faces in the audience.

"I must find just the right person," he said. "But it must be someone very special, with a superior mind. Someone with these psychic abilities himself."

Several of the men eagerly waved their hands but Magnus ignored them. He put his fingers to his temples as if trying to pick up someone's thoughts. Then his face brightened and he whirled about.

"You!" Magnus exclaimed, pointing at the tall figure of Zeb Connelly, who was leaning against a wall. The tall rancher ran his hand through his thinning hair and shook his head. "I can tell you have amazing psychic abilities," said the magician, advancing on him. Zeb held his hands in the air in protest, but Magnus pulled on his arm as the other men whooped and shouted. Finally, Zeb came reluctantly with the little magician to the front of the room. Adrienne brought another chair and waved Zeb toward it. As he sat down, the big bunch of keys at his belt gleamed in the lamplight.

Magnus spoke some hocus-pocus and produced a set of playing cards. Magnus went through a whole series of fast card tricks—having Zeb look at cards which Arabella then guessed. Then Magnus had Zeb draw a card, which was shown to the audience, and Arabella, fingers to her temples in the usual show of capturing mental thought waves, identified it correctly. Finally, Magnus covered Zeb with a sheet and had him pick a card while underneath. Still Arabella guessed right. When Zeb emerged from underneath the sheet and headed back to his place by the wall, Fargo noticed that the big bunch of keys was no longer hanging from Zeb's belt. Great. So far, the plan was working fine.

For the grand finale, Magnus pulled a small lamb out of a seemingly empty crate. The audience whooped and stomped as the magician held the struggling lamb aloft and it bleated a loud protest. After the final bows, Zeb Connelly came forward and Magnus and his daughters excused themselves, saying they were going outside for air. Fargo stayed watching at the window to make sure no one followed them.

Zeb began to recite the expenses and income of the ranch operation as all the men sat forward, listening attentively. Fargo left the window and rounded the ranch house and came to the wide front porch. Magnus and his daughters stood there waiting and looking anxiously out into the darkness.

"Over here," Fargo called in a whisper. Magnus and Arabella hurried over. Adrienne stayed by the front door to divert attention in case anyone happened to come out.

"Here are the keys," Magnus said, pulling them out of his pocket.

"Great," Fargo said, pocketing them. "I watched from the window. That was a terrific show."

"Thank you," the magician said. "I just hope Zeb Connelly doesn't miss those keys anytime soon."

"Yeah," Fargo said. "And I've got some good news for you. There's a little opening in the back of the barn. It's just as I suspected. Your wagon's in there, all right."

Magnus gave a little cry of delight and looked toward the dark, looming shape of the barn. "Let's get it right now!" he said.

"Not so fast," Fargo said. "Let's keep to our plan. Only I've got some more news. Some of it good, some of it bad."

He briefly told Magnus and Arabella the overheard conversation between Zeb and his men, about the burning of Mirage and the planned ambush.

"That's *good* news?" Arabella asked.

"No," Fargo said. "But I expected we'd have to fight it out. Instead, the ranch hands are all away. After the meeting, we'll get the Mirage men rounded up and tell them what's going on. We'll take Zeb Connelly hostage. And I bet Fred is hiding upstairs. Then we'll drive your wagon out of here. But we'll go back to the Piñon Trail by the north route—the way Frederico drove here. That way we'll get back to Mirage and circumvent the ambush waiting on the southern road."

"Clever," Magnus said.

"Only problem is, there won't *be* any Mirage to go back to," Arabella said sadly. There was a long silence.

"What about Juan?" Fargo asked. "What did he have to say?"

"I did just as you told me," Arabella said. "Just after the big supper, I went into the kitchen. But I didn't see anybody who fit your description of him. There was only one fat man with a tattoo on his arm peeling potatoes. So I told him that one of the ranch hands had been bragging about this great Mexican cook named Juan. And I wanted to ask how to make tortillas. The fat man stared at me for a moment like I'd said something wrong. Then he said Juan had gone back to Mexico the week before."

Fargo shook his head in dismay. It was only the day before when the little Mexican man had whispered that he had something to tell him about Frederico. Juan hadn't gone back to Mexico. Juan had undoubtedly been silenced by Zeb Connelly, who had heard him trying to pass on information to Fargo. There was no doubt in Fargo's mind that the Mexican cook was dead.

Just then Fargo heard shouts from inside the ranch house. He instructed Magnus and his daughters to remain on the porch and he sprinted to the window again to find out what was going on inside. Half the Mirage men were on their feet, their fists raised in the air. The others were muttering angrily among themselves. Zeb Connelly held up his hands and shouted for quiet.

"Now look, fellows," Zeb said. "I know this has never happened before. And I know you all came here expecting to go home with your profits in your pockets. But I can't help it if the bank in Cedar City held up the payout."

"Let's get another bank!" one man shouted.

"That's exactly what I'm going to do," Connelly

said smoothly. "I'm riding up to Cedar City tomorrow to take care of it."

"But I thought that payment wagon came through three weeks ago," Eben Blackwell said. "Wasn't all our money in there?"

"Unfortunately, it wasn't," Zeb said. "The bank sent just enough capital to meet our expenses. They promised they will send the rest next week. But that's not good enough for me. And it's not good enough for the co-owners of the Circle C ranch." Zeb stamped his foot for emphasis. "No, sir! I'm going to ride up there tomorrow to take care of the matter personally."

Fargo was astonished. So that was the other part of Zeb's game. The money from the Cedar City bank had probably come in to the ranch like it did every year. Only this time Connelly was pretending it hadn't. And Connelly had planned the whole thing so the Mirage men would be riding off tonight with empty pockets, straight to their deaths. Which would leave Connelly not only with all their livestock but with a full year's profit to boot. Zeb sure had it figured out from every angle, thought Fargo. He grit his teeth as he heard Zeb calming down the group of sheep owners with his lies. Zeb would pay for this, Fargo thought. And soon.

It wasn't long before the meeting was concluded. The disgruntled men got to their feet, donned their hats and jackets, and wandered out into the night air. Fargo, with Zeb's bunch of keys in his pocket, melted away into the darkness near the barn. It wouldn't be long before the men rounded the barn on their way to the corral, which stood nearby. And he'd call them inside to show them the wagon and tell them what was really going on. Then they'd storm the ranch house.

And without the ranch hands around, it would be an easy matter to overpower Zeb and that stinking nephew of his. Fargo smiled to himself. He couldn't wait to witness Zeb's downfall.

Fargo stole around the far side of the barn and pulled out the keys. He tried several of them in the padlock before finding the one that fit. The lock snapped open and Fargo tugged on the huge door. It did not open. Then he remembered the interior bolt. Fargo put his arm through the square hole and groped for the old wooden bar. The bolt shot back with a dull thud. He removed his arm and eased the big door open. It came without a squeak. Fargo slipped inside and struck a match, careful not to let any sparks fall on the floor, which was thick with dry straw.

A metal oil lamp hung on a post by a nail. For a moment, he wondered if the light would spill through the walls. But the massive wooden barn was solidly built, with double walls, no chinks, and no windows. The light wouldn't be seen from the ranch house. He lit the wick and turned it up high, then went outside again and waited for the Mirage men to start walking toward the corral. He heard Zeb Connelly bidding everyone good night. Then the ranch-house door slammed shut. Now was his chance. But he'd have to move quickly and quietly.

Not surprisingly, Magnus and his daughters appeared first and slipped inside the barn with excitement. He heard their muffled exclamations of delight as they saw their treasured wagon of tricks again. A few other men ambled by and Fargo called out to them. Eben Blackwell was among them.

"You're being cheated," Fargo said quietly to Eben.

"Round up the rest of the men, but be quiet about it. Get everybody into the barn. It's life or death."

Blackwell moved off to do his bidding as Fargo thought again of Hank Giffin. Life or death. Yes, Hank had used those very words in his last telegram. Fargo stood just outside the barn door, warning everyone to be silent as they entered. When the last one of the men was inside, he slipped in and pulled the door mostly closed behind him.

"Zeb Connelly's cheating you," Fargo said, his voice low. A few men began talking, and the others, realizing the gravity of the situation, shushed them. "Not only that, he's sent his ranch hands off tonight to burn up the town." There was a low mutter.

"I don't believe this," one man said in a loud voice.

"Quiet," Fargo said, his voice low. "Did anybody notice something strange tonight? Zeb Connelly invited Magnus the Magnificent to do a show especially for his ranch hands tonight. But none of them even showed up." There was a shocked silence as all the men took in his words. Then several nodded thoughtfully.

"And right now they're lying in wait on the southern road," Fargo continued. "They're going to ambush you and make it look like the Hopis did it."

Several men started to protest in disbelief but then stopped themselves.

"You telling us that Zeb is behind the murder of Hank Giffin?" one man asked, leaping ahead to put two and two together.

"Damn right," Fargo said. "Hank found out about Zeb's plan. Only Zeb got to him before he could get enough evidence. And Zeb's been killing Hopis, too, trying to scare them off their land."

"What the hell can we do about it?" Blackwell asked.

In the momentary silence, Fargo heard a sound behind him—the whisper of a sound, a footfall on the ground. The significance of it suddenly struck him and he whirled about an instant too late. He saw the huge door of the barn swinging shut. He threw his full weight against the heavy wood, but at that moment he heard the snap of the padlock and a sickeningly cruel laugh, which went on and on. There wasn't a sound inside the barn as each of them took in what had just happened.

"There's nothing you can do about it," Zeb Connelly's voice shouted. And he laughed again.

Fargo drew his Colt and stepped up to the small square hole to try to get a shot at Zeb. But the wily rancher had obviously considered this, and Fargo heard his footsteps hurrying around the corner of the barn. Fargo stepped back and wondered how thick the double walls were and whether they would stop a bullet.

"What luck," Connelly called out, his voice distant. Fargo could just make out the words through the thick walls. "Every one of you stupid bastards locked up tight!"

Yeah, hardly, Fargo thought. He absently patted his pocket, which held the keys to the padlock. All they had to do was wait for Connelly to walk away, and he'd have them free in a minute.

"So, you're planning to cheat us, Connelly," Blackwell shouted, rage in his voice.

"Just clearing out the riffraff," Connelly said. Fargo stepped back as he listened. He could tell from Zeb's voice exactly where he was standing now, just to the right of the corner of the barn. Fargo raised his Colt and fired—once, twice, three times. One of Magnus's daughters screamed, and the other men instinctively drew their pistols, too. There was silence outside and inside. Fargo began to hope. Maybe he'd plugged the bastard. He advanced to the bullet holes in the wooden walls and saw that, although the slugs had passed through the thinner interior walls, they were embedded in the thick outer walls. The goddamned barn was built like a fortress.

"Good try, Fargo," Zeb said. His voice had moved to another side of the barn, away from the doors. "That *was* you, wasn't it?"

"Yeah, that was me," Fargo said, advancing to the square hole and shouting through it. He couldn't see into the blackness and he knew that Zeb was too clever to come into his line of fire. He wished Zeb would just clear off so he could get down to unlocking the padlock. Just then, Fargo heard the sound of another voice, a familiar voice, calling softly from what seemed like the direction of the ranch house.

"Uncle Zeb? Uncle Zeb?" It was Fred, Fargo realized. Sounding scared. "I heard gunshots!" Then he added, still in a low voice, "They're all gone, aren't they?"

"Hell, no," Connelly answered his nephew. "I got 'em all locked up in the barn. And now I'm going to make them dance!"

Fargo, his ear pressed to the square opening, didn't like the sound of that. He doubted if the others had heard the two quiet voices. For a moment, he wondered if he should let Adrienne know that her former fiancé was right outside.

"Well," Zeb shouted in a loud voice for the benefit

of those inside the barn. "I just want to thank all you boys from Mirage for making me a very wealthy man." He had moved again, Fargo noticed, to the side of the barn where the haystack was. There was a long silence as everyone in the barn waited. Then Fargo heard a crackling sound. He put his face to the opening. At first there was nothing to be seen, but he immediately smelled trouble in the cold night air. Smoke. Burning hay. And almost immediately he could see the flicker of the flames.

"Hey! You can't do that!" Frederico shouted, loud enough to be heard by everyone in the barn. "You can't just burn people up!"

"What's going on?" Blackwell shouted.

"Zeb's set fire to the haystack by the barn," Fargo said, turning around to address them. His attention was drawn by Adrienne, whose face held a mixture of horror and recognition.

"Fred?" she screamed. "Fred? It's me! Adrienne!"

"You can't do this!" Fred shrieked when he heard her voice.

The crackle of fire could be heard already. Everyone in the barn began to mutter as the implication hit them. Fargo pressed his ear to the opening and listened intently to what was going on outside. He heard the sound of a brief struggle. Adrienne stole up beside him and he moved a little so that she could hear as well.

"Come on, Fred," Zeb said after a moment. "You knew we were going to do away with these people."

"But not . . . not . . ." Fred said.

"Plenty more where she came from," Zeb snapped. "Stop being such a wimp."

"Then what about the wagon? What about my career as a magician?"

"Have you got that stuff you used yesterday at the mesa?"

"It's packed on the mules," Frederico answered.

"Then let the rest burn," Zeb said. "Forget this sissy show business stuff. Tonight will make a real man out of you. We're heading out at dawn to clean out that stinking Indian village. When word gets out that those Hopis burned down the town of Mirage and my barn with all the townsfolk inside, then nobody will blame us for slaughtering those savages once and for all." Fred started to protest again, but Zeb cut in. "Now come on, Fred. It's time for you to learn to be a real man. Time for you to learn how to kill. But first we're going to fetch the boys and call off the ambush."

Adrienne sagged against him. Fargo listened, hearing the footsteps of Zeb and Fred grow fainter. After a half minute, he heard the sound of two horses galloping fast along the road.

By now the fire was roaring outside. In moments the whole place would go up. At that moment, almost everyone began to panic. Men started to hurl themselves against the doors. Magnus stood to one side, drawing his daughters close. Someone, in a rush to throw himself against the barn wall, knocked into the oil lamp and Fargo saw it go askew. He leaped for it and managed to catch it before it overturned and set fire to the straw on the floor. He handed it to Blackwell, who was standing nearby.

"Hold it!" Fargo shouted. "Keep calm!" But it was in vain. The smell of smoke was filtering into the barn and the roar of the raging fire increased. He could already feel the heat on the side of the barn near the burning hay. It wouldn't be long before the roof caught fire and collapsed on top of them. But long before that happened, a spark would fall and ignite the hay inside the barn. They would all be fried in an instantaneous explosion of fire. Fargo pulled the keys out of his pocket, but there were so many men desperately trying to break down the heavy wooden doors that he couldn't get near the opening. He shouted for them to get back and dragged them away bodily.

"I've got keys!" he shouted, trying to make himself understood in the panic. Several of the more level-headed men who were standing to the rear understood and helped him move the others aside. Fargo hugged the door and, with the keys in hand, passed his arm through the small opening and fumbled for the padlock. He found it, but it was farther than he had expected. At once, he realized it was going to be almost impossible to insert the key into the tight lock with only one hand. But he had to. Their lives depended on it.

The air thickened with smoke. The men moved down to the other end of the barn, where they tried in vain to batter down the thick doors. Everyone was coughing. While he tried to get the key into the lock, Fargo glanced over to see the little magician and his daughters huddled near the ground, where the air was clearer. The women held handkerchiefs over their mouths, and their wide eyes were scared.

Again and again, he pushed the key into the edge of the padlock and pushed it upward, only to have the heavy lock slip to one side. Fargo swore. He swore loudly at Zeb Connelly, at his thieving nephew Frederico, and the two-hearted Hopi, Running Dog. With a final burst of energy he tried once again, jamming the key upward into the lock. His hands were sweating with the effort and the heat. Suddenly, he lost his grip on the ring of keys and it slipped from his grasp.

He heard the sound of the keys hitting the ground outside the barn door, way out of reach. And at the same moment, he heard the crackle of flames on the roof above. They were doomed.

7

For a brief instant, Fargo leaned against the thick wooden door in despair. Smoke filled his nose and lungs. The keys lay on the ground, well out of reach. How the hell could he get them? He thought of the Ovaro, waiting at the edge of the woods. Fargo puckered his lips and whistled—a low but piercing sound that carried a long way. He wondered if the faithful pinto would hear his whistle over the roar of the fire. In a moment, he heard the horse gallop up to the barn, but he doubted if it would help. The pinto was intelligent . . . but smart enough to pick up keys?

In the wavering firelight, he spotted the Ovaro as it galloped toward the burning barn. Not one horse in a thousand would come straight toward a fire, he thought with gratitude. He put his arm through the opening and heard it whinny, then felt its warm muzzle on his hand. How could he communicate what he wanted? The horse, made skittish by the flames, backed off and snorted. Fargo pointed downward toward the ground, hoping the horse would spot the keys. But instead the pinto gave a shrill neigh. It began to pound the door with its hooves in a vain attempt to break down the door and set him free. Good try, Fargo said silently to his faithful horse. But he knew even the powerful hooves of his Ovaro were no match for the stout doors.

"What's going on?" Magnus said, drawing near. Several of the men nearby listened for his answer. They were all coughing in the dense smoke. Most had tied bandannas over nose and mouth. Fargo didn't want to admit he'd dropped the keys. All they needed was more panic.

"I've almost got it," Fargo said encouragingly. He had a sudden idea to keep everybody busy. "Get this hay on the floor pushed against the far end!" he shouted. "One spark and we're all goners!" The men saw the wisdom of this, and in seconds they were pushing the hay toward the other end of the barn, leaving the earth floor bare. Magnus remained by Fargo's elbow.

"Let me try it," he said in a low voice.

"I dropped the keys," Fargo admitted in a low voice.

"I know," Magnus said as a look passed between them. "I recognize a good performance when I see one."

Fargo drew in his arm. Magnus fished in his pocket and drew forth a fishhooklike apparatus on a long, thin wire. Fargo wondered which trick he used that for. The pinto continued to beat against the door. Just then, Fargo heard a sound from above—the crackle of burning wood. He watched as a shower of sparks floated down onto the floor where only moments before had been a thick layer of straw. The coughing men, having finished moving the hay, gathered around the door. The short magician couldn't quite reach through the opening. Fargo lifted him a few inches, and in a second, Magnus had his hand through the hole, a look of concentration on his face. Fargo was just wondering if the little man's arm was long enough to reach the padlock when he heard the metallic snap of the lock. A big smile crossed Magnus's face. He pulled in his hand. In it was the open padlock.

With an excited cheer, the men surged forward against the doors. They heaved them open and a rush of cold, clear air rushed into the barn. The Mirage men were pouring out just as Fargo heard another one of the roof supports creak ominously above him. It looked ready to give way. Just then, falling sparks hit on the pile of hay now at the other end of the barn. The straw exploded in a flash of light, throwing the interior of the barn into high relief and silhouetting the painted wagon.

"My wagon! My wagon!" Magnus shrieked. He pushed his daughters out the doors and turned to go back inside. Fargo followed. After the little magician had saved their lives, he'd be damned if he'd let Magnus kill himself trying to rescue a bunch of magic tricks.

"Magnus!" Fargo shouted, his voice harsh from the smoke. He sprinted after him into the smoke and flaming interior. The magician had reached the wagon and grasped one of the shafts. He pulled, trying desperately to drag the wagon out of the barn. Showers of sparks rained down around them as Fargo grabbed the little man and tried to pull him away to safety.

"No!" Magnus shouted above the roar of the fire. He refused to let go of the shaft. "This is my life!" It was useless to argue. The flames from the burning pile of hay were licking the roof inside, only hastening its collapse. Any second now, the whole thing would go. Fargo seized the other shaft and pulled hard. After a second, the mountain wagon began to inch forward.

Part of the roof behind them collapsed. Fargo could feel the heat searing his skin and hair. He glanced at Magnus and saw him wince at the blasting fire, his gray eyebrows badly singed. Still, they remained with the wagon, pulling the heavy load inch by inch.

Above the crackling and roaring of the fire, Fargo heard the men outside screaming at them to give up and save themselves. Then the Ovaro came galloping through the open doors. But there was no time to put it into the traces and Fargo shooed it out again. Eben Blackwell dashed in and put his shoulder to the wheel. The wagon moved faster. Three more men braved the flames and dashed in to help. The shafts of the wagon reached the door. Other men crowded up and pulled at the wagon, which was moving fast now. Just as the rear of the wagon cleared the barn doors, the roof collapsed in a huge heave of sparks. A massive explosion of fire vaulted into the night sky and a tower of smoke obscured the stars. The flames licked them as they pulled and pushed the wagon beyond the reach of the fire.

Once they were clear and out in the meadow, they halted. Fargo drew deep draughts of the fresh air into his aching lungs. The skin on his face was painfully blistered and cracked. He put his hand to his scalp and felt the curl of his singed hair. But hell, he was alive, he thought. They were all alive.

"Skye! Thank you!" Arabella said, hugging him. She looked a sight, her face charred and her hair a wild mass.

"Three cheers for Fargo!" a man nearby shouted.

"Hold on!" Fargo called out. "It was Magnus who saved our lives."

So the men cheered them both and Fargo let them have their moment of celebration—because there was still a long night ahead of them. They weren't safe and it wasn't over yet. After a few minutes, Fargo quieted them.

"I heard Zeb Connelly say he was heading out to fetch the men who were waiting to ambush you," he said. "They'll be back here any minute. I want everybody to get on his horse right now. Just beyond this rise is a small meadow. Wait for me there. And some of you men pull this wagon up the hill and into that pine grove. Hide it well." Magnus started to protest at the idea of his precious wagon being left behind, but Fargo held up his hand. "The wagon will be safe there until morning," Fargo said to the magician. "And this is life or death."

The men, all with burns and charred hair, did as they were told. In minutes, they'd hidden the wagon and led their nervous horses out of the corral and up the hill. Magnus and his two daughters went along. Fargo stayed behind to make sure everyone got away. He carefully left the corral gate wide open. If Zeb or his men noticed that the horses were gone, they would assume they'd wandered off. When the last of the men were headed up the sloping meadow toward cover, Fargo mounted the Ovaro. He patted the trusty pinto's neck and felt the roughness of its singed coat. Then he turned and galloped up the hill.

While the others made their way through the dark woods to the meadow, Fargo stood watch over the ranch and the burning barn. The flames had died down, but a red-gold fire burned steadily. From time to time, blackened timbers fell into the flames and a shower of sparks rose in the still night air. From the confused jumble of burning wreckage, it was impossible to tell they had escaped.

Fifteen minutes later, Fargo heard the pounding of hooves. A dark crowd of riders came speeding down the road. As they passed the burning barn, they whooped and cheered. Bastards, Fargo thought. He watched as one man dismounted in front of the ranch house and went inside. Zeb Connelly, Fargo thought. Another smaller figure followed—probably Frederico. For a long time, Fargo remained motionless. He stared at the golden-windowed ranch house as if his gaze alone could set it on fire. After a few minutes, he saw a figure at one of the lighted windows upstairs. The man stood looking toward the smoldering ruin of the barn. But whether it was the remorseful Fred, or Zeb Connelly enjoying his supposed victory, Fargo never knew. At that moment, he turned away and plunged into the forest.

What had finally convinced them were the numbers, thought Fargo as he hunched beside the tangle of sagebrush, waiting for the coming of dawn. Sunrise was still an hour away, and the attack would come an hour after that. He pushed aside the fragrant branches and peered out into the starlit darkness. His eyes picked out the compact figure of Bear Paw sitting a couple of feet from him. With slow, steady motions, the old man was intent on sharpening the blade of his long knife. Beyond him, Eben Blackwell sat uncomfortably on the ground. When Blackwell heard the rustle of motion from Fargo's direction, he glanced over at him. Even in the near-darkness, Fargo could read Blackwell's expression and knew what he was thinking: White men aren't supposed to fight side by side with Indians. But they did, thought Fargo, when they were badly outnumbered . . . and they had a common enemy.

It had been hard going back in the dark meadow to convince the angry men of Mirage not to simply swoop back down on the Circle C ranch right then and wreak their revenge. They were outnumbered two to one, Fargo pointed out. When he announced he had a better plan, they listened. But when they realized he was asking them to join forces with the Hopis when the ranch hands attacked the mesa at dawn, many protested. Fargo used all his persuasive powers to make them see that swallowing their prejudice and their pride would save their lives. And finally they agreed.

Then Fargo had led them through the dark forest and across the meadows. He made them cross the ranch road one by one in case any of Connelly's men happened to be straggling back from the intended ambush site. But they met no one. Then he led them bushwhacking northward, where they at last joined the Piñon Trail and followed it into the smoking ruin of Mirage. To their surprise, a few shacks had escaped the fire. Magnus asked if his daughters might remain behind, but Fargo told him they'd all be safer up on the mesa.

Fargo drove them on. Exhausted and singed, they nevertheless galloped fast, eastward down the long slope and into the wide Hopi lands. Fargo heard the coyotes singing to the stars. He was glad there was no moon. They'd need darkness. Several hours before dawn, they drew near the Hopi mesa. M____ _f the men, who had never ventured this far into the Indian lands, gasped at the magnitude of the looming butte. They passed the abandoned ranch and the creek. Then Fargo halted and told them all to stay behind while he approached the path up to the pueblo. He had gone only a few hundred yards when he heard a whisper of movement.

"Friend," Fargo said in the Hopi dialect. "I am Skye Fargo."

A dark figure stepped out from behind a rock and Fargo recognized the broad, strong outlines of Fire Dawn. For a moment, his heart sank. Fire Dawn had believed the *kachina* messages absolutely. But had Sun-Sky's murder changed his mind? And would he believe Fargo that white men were coming to attack, but that other white men would fight alongside the Hopis?

"Wanderer Friend," Fire Dawn addressed Fargo, "today Bear Paw saw with his invisible eye that you would come in the night. The old man said you would bring white friends. You are welcome."

Fargo brought the pinto nearer Fire Dawn, bent down, and offered his hand to the standing brave. Fargo knew that by his few simple words, Fire Dawn was saying he had been wrong about the *kachina* messages. Wrong insisting that the tribe had to go south to the Red City. And wrong about Bear Paw's powers. But more words were not necessary at such a moment. Fargo clasped the brave's warm hand and held it for a long moment. Then he straightened up on his horse.

"I will lead the white friends up onto the mesa," Fargo said. "And then we will plan for battle."

The ████ braves were ready for them, waiting at

the top of the path in full battle regalia. The women hurried forward and when they saw what was needed brought herb salves and bandages for the burns and cuts. Arabella and Adrienne were led away to rest at the pueblo. Fargo told Magnus to go with the women and remain there.

"You've saved our lives already tonight, Magnus," Fargo said. "You've already won your battle." But Magnus insisted that he might be valuable if Frederico tried the *kachina* trick again. And finally, Fargo relented.

And now they were all sitting in the sage, keeping silent watch over the ghost ranch and the creek, waiting for the light to come. The Hopis had supplied each man with a tangle of sagebrush that had been cleverly tied together to form a dense enclosure. Each man could hide in the center, hunched down. And if he moved slowly enough, anybody watching would not catch on that there was anyone there or that the bush was slowly moving.

It was still well before dawn. Fargo was surprised when he heard the first signal—a single coyote yip from the distance of a quarter mile. That was the call of the most distant watchers. They had already spotted someone moving in. Why the hell was the attack coming so early? Were the ranch hands moving into position already? All around him in the darkness came the slight rustle of sage branches, like the stirring of wind, as the Hopi and Mirage men alike hunched down into their camouflage. Then all was still.

Ten minutes later, through the sage branches, Fargo saw a dark figure darting toward the creek. He deposited something on the bank and then disappeared again in the darkness. Fargo sat perfectly still, hardly breathing as the moments passed. Then he heard the signal again from far away and he relaxed. Whoever it was—and Fargo wondered if it had been Running Dog—had slipped in to leave another *kachina* message by the creek. Fargo had no doubt the pictures on the rock would promise a *kachina* appearance that very morning. Only this time, Connelly's men would be waiting to attack.

An hour later, right on schedule and just as the sky was brightening with the predawn light, he heard the coyote calls—several mournful wails. The signal that Connelly's men were moving into position now, creeping through the sage lying around the mesa. As he waited, Fargo rechecked the bullets in his Colt and his Sharps rifle. His pockets and belt were full of extra ammunition. After a few minutes, he heard the cackling alarm call of the burrowing owl, a two-note coo that meant the ranch hands were moving into the near position. He eyed the nubby sage plain and caught sight of the smallest flickers—a branch snapping back, the subtle sway of a bush against the breeze, as the attackers crawled straight toward them. Time for the next part of the battle plan.

Behind him, Fargo immediately heard the sound of running feet and boys' voices shouting excitedly as they ran down the path. The boys knew what role they had to play in this battle. It was possible that one or all of them could be shot. But to any of the ranch hands crawling through the sage, the boys would have sounded perfectly natural. Only Connelly wouldn't have expected them to descend from the mesa so early. Running Dog would have told him the boys usually came for water after sunrise, not before. But this was part of Fargo's plan. He wanted Connelly's men to be caught short, so they wouldn't have time to get themselves completely into position. Instead, they'd be pinned down and all spread out.

Fargo watched as the boys ran toward the creek. One of them shrieked in pretended surprise when he spotted the rock. Only this time, instead of all the boys running back up the trail with the rock, only one went. The others remained behind, looking around and peering up at the ledge where the *kachina* had appeared the day before. This was the trickiest moment, Fargo thought. It was in the next few minutes that they would succeed or fail. The boys continued to jump up and down in excitement, trying to draw the attention of Connelly's men, lying unseen in the sage and unable to move further forward without being spotted by the boys.

Fargo rose to his toes and, holding the sage around him, moved very slowly away from the mesa. All around him, the Hopis and the Mirage men were moving into position, gradually easing closer to where the ranch hands were hiding in the sage. Far out to the left, Fargo knew, a group of Hopis led by Fire Dawn was swinging around behind, crawling through the brush to mount a rear attack on the ranch hands. Connelly's men were undoubtedly going crazy in the brush. They hadn't gained the best position to attack the Hopis, who would gather on the bank of the creek. And they couldn't move for fear of being spotted by the sharp-eyed Indian boys.

Fifteen long minutes later, Fargo had moved a dozen slow yards. Ten feet away, he caught sight of a round back and a hat—a ranch hand hunched in the brush. Fargo stopped short. No use getting closer, he thought. Once the fun started, he could shoot from here perfectly well. He wondered where Zeb Connelly was and hoped he'd get his hands on him in the middle of the coming fracas.

From the direction of the mesa, Fargo heard the sound of excited voices and high-pitched laughter. The next phase of the plan was about to begin. Hurrying down the path came a crowd of Hopis. The braves rushed along, shouting happily to one another. The knives which usually swung at their belts were hidden inside their shirts. Many of the women had volunteered to go as well. They walked stiffly, hiding rifles in their skirts and draped serapes. Fargo saw the tall figure of Raindrop among them. There was no lack of courage among any of the Hopi people, Fargo thought admiringly. The Indians hurried to the bank of the creek, shouting and laughing in anticipation of seeing the *kachina* again. Fargo hoped Connelly and his men wouldn't stop to wonder why there were no small children in the group.

A few minutes later, a shout of excitement came from those waiting at the creek and Fargo knew it meant that Frederico had once again created the illusion of the *kachina* spirit dancing in the sky above the rock ledge. From within the cover of the sage, Fargo couldn't see the *kachina*. But he knew its appearance was the signal for attack.

Suddenly, a man shouted from out in the sage. Immediately, Connelly's men popped up from the brush and began firing toward the creek, trying to mow down the group of Hopis. The man near Fargo rose to his knees and began firing. From within the sage, Fargo brought up his Colt and picked off the man easily. Fargo spotted another of Connelly's men, who rose above the sage to fire, and he shot him in the head. He plugged two more in quick succession.

All around, there were shrieks of surprise and horror as Connelly's men popped up out of the brush only to find that their intended victims had thrown themselves into the slight depression of the creek bed, out of the line of fire. And it was impossible to move forward without being gunned down mysteriously from close range. Connelly's men shouted to each other, many calling for a retreat. The ranks of the ranch hands had already been devastated. Over the melee, Fargo heard two voices nearby, and he slowly moved his sage bush until he came up behind two men hunched side by side.

"What the hell's going on?" one asked.

"Damned if I know," the other muttered. "Zeb said this would be a piece of cake. He said we'd slaughter them. Just like last night."

At those words, Fargo felt the rage well in him. Last night? When the returning ranch hands had cheered to see the burned-out barn where they supposed so many innocent men had died? Despite his anger, Fargo couldn't shoot two men in the back in cold blood. With a cry of rage, he sprang from the bush, intending to throttle them. He landed on one of the men and knocked the wind clean out of him. The other, with a second's warning, brought his pistol around, but Fargo deflected it with his forearm just as it went off. The bullet flew wide and Fargo drew back his fist. He sank a hard right into the man's face and felt the jawbone crunch under his knuckles. The man's head snapped backward and he collapsed. The anger subsided in Fargo, hardened to black revenge. The first man struggled to regain his breath just as Fargo, Colt in hand, coldcocked him.

Behind him, Fargo heard shouts and gunfire. The rear attack was beginning. A wave of confusion passed through Connelly's men as they realized the enemy was not only among them but was sweeping up their backside as well. The panic spread through the ranks and many of the ranch hands got to their feet, hands in the air. Fargo's eyes swept them, looking in vain for the tall figure in gray. Not there. The battle would be over in a few minutes. The lines of Hopi and Mirage men were sweeping toward one another and would close in on what was left of Connelly's men like deadly pincers. He wasn't needed here, Fargo thought.

He sprinted through the sage and leaped down into the creek depression. He paused a moment to look over the Indians huddled there. Only a few of them had been hit in the first volley before they vaulted into the cover of the creek bed. Two braves had shoulder wounds and one of the women sat with lips tight, having taken a bullet in the leg. Raindrop, Fargo was relieved to see, was fine. The boys who had created the diversion were trying to catch sight of the enemy. Fargo told them they had been great warriors and they broke out in smiles.

Then Fargo ran on past the deserted ranch, heading for the path leading up to the rock ledge. Magnus was waiting for him by the big rock. Fargo was surprised to see Bear Paw there, too. The little magician was looking up at the ledge. He pointed excitedly. Fargo was surprised to see that the *kachina* still hovered above the ledge in midair. Surely Frederico could see that the battle was lost and that he ought to make a run for it. On the other hand, how many battles had the magician ever seen? And where the hell would he run? Fargo stared upward for another moment. From this vantage point, the illusion didn't look quite right. The sky seemed bent and rocks cropped out under the *kachina's* dancing legs.

"Shoot," Magnus said. "Shoot right there under his feet."

Fargo raised his Sharps and aimed at a spot a few inches below the *kachina*. At this distance, it was impossible to be entirely accurate. But so what if Frederico lost a few toes. . . .

Fargo fired. The sky seemed to explode and shatter beneath the floating *kachina*. The black-and-white figure leaped up in surprise. And then Fargo saw that the *kachina* was standing on some kind of platform. The illusion had disappeared. As Fargo watched, he saw the *kachina* tear off its mask, revealing a small bald head. It was definitely Frederico.

Several of the men from Mirage were ascending the path to the south, Fargo knew. A moment later, Fargo heard gunfire. And then, far above at the edge of the rock ledge, he saw the scared face of Frederico appear. Fargo ran forward, followed by Magnus and Bear Paw, as the magician started to climb down the steep rock face, feeling for the hand- and toe-holds. Suddenly, he looked down and spotted them approaching from below. He was trapped and he knew it. Frederico clung to the rock for a long moment. Then he let go and leaned back into space. He plummeted through the emptiness. He fell heavily onto the rocks below, bounced, and dropped out of sight. A coward's death, Fargo thought.

"Stay here," Fargo told Magnus and Bear Paw. The old Hopi man nodded and took a seat on a nearby rock, patting the stone beside him and indicating that

Magnus should sit, too. Fargo sprinted around the base of the mesa through the huge red boulders toward the other path to the ledge. He still hadn't spotted Zeb Connelly. Or Running Dog. And he wondered where they were.

As he rounded a boulder and came to the open place where Sun-Sky had been killed, Fargo stopped short. Tethered to a cliffrose bush was Zeb Connelly's ebony stallion. He'd have known it anywhere. Fargo backed up quickly and ducked behind a rock, Colt in hand. He listened but heard only a few voices from the ledge far above. The Mirage men were combing the path for any stragglers from Connelly's band.

Fargo stood, puzzled for a moment, wondering where the hell Zeb Connelly had got to. Then, from behind him, he heard the whisper of gravel. In a split second, Fargo jumped away as the bullet whined by, grazing his cheek. As he hit the ground and rolled, one dark thought came into his mind. Zeb Connelly had sneaked up on him for the last time.

Fargo came up to one knee, Colt blazing, only to find that Connelly was nowhere in sight. A jumble of red rocks met his gaze. In an instant, he threw himself behind a rock, but not before a second bullet exploded and he felt a jolt of pain as the slug tore through his thigh. Hell, Fargo told himself, he wasn't going anywhere now. He couldn't dash forward on his leg. But at least he knew where Connelly was hidden, Fargo thought as he gritted his teeth and reloaded. The shot had come from behind a boulder stuck in a crevice. Fargo's eyes flitted upward for a moment and he smiled to himself. He pulled up his Sharps and his Colt and regarded the rocks again with narrowed eyes. It just might work, he thought. But it would take all six bullets in his Colt and the one in his Sharps, fired in quick succession.

Fargo aimed carefully at the huge rock balanced up above the crevice where Connelly was hunkered down. He raised the rifle and fired. The bullet smashed into the small rocks beneath, which held the boulder balanced. His Colt was in his hand and he fired once, twice, six times fast. The small rocks shattered, the boulder teetered and rocked forward into the crevice. Fargo heard a bloodcurdling shriek as the boulder crashed forward and cracked apart.

Fargo reloaded his Colt in an instant. Then he knotted his neckerchief around his leg and tightened it with a stick to stop the bleeding. The leg wouldn't take any weight, but with the aid of a bent stick, he got to his feet and moved slowly and painfully toward the rock crevice, pistol in hand. A huge portion of the boulder lay across Zeb Connelly's midsection. The rancher's face was ashen and a stream of bright blood ran from his gaping mouth. Fargo thought he was dead. But then Connelly's eyelids fluttered open.

"Why'd you do it, Connelly?" Fargo asked.

The man's lips moved but no sound came. He blinked unseeingly and made another effort. This time a few words came out.

"Ranch. My father's ranch. Goddamn . . . redskins . . . ran him off. . . ."

The muscles in the hard planes of Zeb Connelly's face suddenly slackened and the eyes went blank. Fargo stood looking down at him for a long time. So, the ghost ranch had belonged to Connelly's father. Fargo suspected that no Connelly would have been a welcome neighbor. Especially so close to a pueblo where the Hopis had lived for generations. And so the

Hopis had forced Zeb's father to move away. Killed him, maybe. And Zeb Connelly had spent all his life figuring out his revenge.

As Fargo moved away from the body, several Mirage men came running, having heard the gunfire. They helped him up onto Connelly's stallion and Fargo headed back to the place where he'd left Magnus and Bear Paw. There was no sound from the direction of the creek. The battle was long since over and Connelly's men were undoubtedly rounded up.

Fargo found Bear Paw and Magnus still sitting together on the rock. The Hopi was looking through his crystal while Magnus watched in fascination. Bear Paw lowered it and glanced at the magician.

"I see a white woman face," Bear Paw said, struggling for the few words he knew in English. "Black hair. And a . . ." The old man paused helplessly, touching his face with one finger right beside his nose.

"A spot?" Magnus said. "A mole?" His voice rose excitedly.

"And dress the color of spring grass," Bear Paw continued.

"That's my Alice. My wife!" Magnus said. He added softly, "Dead eighteen years."

"She sends you message. She says stop looking," Bear Paw said gravely. Magnus nodded seriously and then noticed Fargo's presence. He glanced at him.

"I think I'm going to live here for a while," Magnus said. "With the Hopi. I think I found something better than magic."

Fargo smiled and rode on as the two old men continued to talk together.

* * *

"Does that hurt?" Arabella asked as she gently stroked his thigh near the bandage over his bullet wound. It had been only five days, but Fargo could already feel the wound closing and the strength in his leg returning. Another week or two and he knew he'd have to ride on. Everything was cleared up now. Connelly's men had been sent to the jail in Cedar City. And most of the men in Mirage were staying at the ranch until they could rebuild the town.

Only one thing bothered Fargo. He never had found Running Dog. Somehow, the sly Indian had slipped away. Fargo hoped he was gone for good. But for now, Fargo was content to be occupying one of the only shacks left in Mirage while Arabella pampered him.

He reached over and pulled her toward him. The golden morning sun poured in the window and splashed across the bed. The light in her dark hair glistened like black diamonds. He kissed her lightly and heard a knock at the door. Adrienne's head appeared, her face all smiles.

"Eben and I are going off for a ride," she announced. "He's going to show me his sheep."

Fargo laughed as she shut the door. Arabella's sweet mouth pouted for a moment and Fargo chucked her under the chin.

"She's got Eben . . ." Arabella said.

"That's my price," Fargo said. "You know I move on. Let's just enjoy the time we've got." Arabella nodded, smiled again, and nestled next to him.

"You know I'd do anything for you, Skye," she murmured. He glanced over at her and took in the lovely swells of her full breasts and the curve of full hips.

"Well, there *is* something, come to think of it."

"Name it."

"Tell me . . . just how does that Wondrous Floating Lady trick work?"

Arabella sat up and threw a pillow at him. Fargo made a grab for her and tickled her ribs.

"Mirrors!" she gasped, between bouts of laughter. "But . . . I won't tell you more!"

"I have ways to make you talk," he said.

LOOKING FORWARD!
The following is the opening
section from the next novel in the exciting
Trailsman series from Signet:

**THE TRAILSMAN #158
TEXAS TERROR**

*1860, deep in Texas, where the sun
is hotter, the women wilder, and the
killers all have itchy trigger fingers . . .*

The small town of Ripclaw was just like any other in
the state of Texas. Or so Skye Fargo thought as his
weary pinto stallion plodded up the middle of the
dusty main street. Few people were abroad in the blis-
tering heat of the late afternoon. He saw an elderly
couple come out of the general store and a pair of
young women in tight-fitting dresses sashay toward a
grimy saloon.

At the livery Fargo reined up. Easing his tired body
to the ground, he pulled his heavy-caliber Sharps from
its doeskin saddle scabbard and led the Ovaro into the
cool interior. "Anybody here?" he called out.

From the murky shadows at the rear emerged a
scarecrow of a man in patched overalls, a sliver of
straw jutting from the corner of his thin mouth. Hook-
ing his thumbs in frayed suspenders, he said, "Howdy,
stranger. I'm Eli and I run the place. What can I do for
you?"

"I'd like to put my horse up for the night," Fargo said, taking the stallion to an empty stall. "Give him some feed, some water, and a rubdown. I'll be by at first light."

"Sure thing, pardner," Eli said, leaning on a post while studying the pinto. "That's a right fine animal you've got there, if you don't mind my saying so. And I know, 'cause horseflesh is my stock and trade." He spat the straw out. "Looks like you've been on the go a spell."

"Two days," Fargo said. He didn't bother to mention it had been two days with little food and no sleep. "I saw a hotel on the way in. Is it worth staying at?"

"The Imperial? Shucks, yes. The lady who owns it prides herself on having a clean, upstanding establishment. I hear tell she changes the bedding once a week, whether the beds need changing or not. And the food she serves is enough to make a single man want to dig in roots."

Fargo leaned his rifle against the stall and removed his bedroll and saddlebags. As he began stripping off his saddle, Eli came forward.

"No need to do that, mister. I can see you're plumb tuckered out. Leave the rig to me. I'll store it in the tack room till morning."

"Thanks." Fargo made for the double doors, draping the saddlebags over his right shoulders. Under his left arm went the bedroll. He was almost to the bright sunlight when the owner called out.

"In case my helper is here in the morning and not me, I'll need a name to tell him. Who might you be?"

"Fargo."

"What?"

"Skye Fargo."

Striding into the harsh glare, Fargo thought he heard an odd gurgling sound and glanced back. Eli was as rigid as a board, his dark eyes as wide as walnuts. "Is anything wrong?" Fargo asked.

"No, sir!" Eli blurted. "Ain't nothing the matter at all! Had a lump in my throat, is all. You go on about your business and I'll tend to your pinto."

Fargo nodded, then made for the Imperial, his boots raising puffs of dust, his spurs jangling. He pulled his hat brim lower to shield his face. The only thing moving outside the hotel was a solitary fly, which he swatted aside as he gripped the door handle. About to go in, he happened to glance toward the stable and saw Eli bolting across the street as if the devil himself were in pursuit. Strange man, Fargo reflected.

The lobby was comfortably furnished. Potted plants, drapes, and doilies showed a woman's touch. Fargo crossed to the front desk and tapped the top of a small bell beside the register.

A curtain parted and out strolled a stunning brunette in a green frilly dress, barely less revealing than those of the saloon girls. She blinked on seeing him, then smiled suggestively and leaned on the countertop, showing more of her already ample cleavage. "Why, hello handsome. Haven't seen you around before. I'm Eleanor Seaver, but most folks call me Ellen."

"I'm told you have a fine hotel here," Fargo said, setting down his bedroll.

Ellen smirked. "Well, I don't mean to brag, but you won't find a cleaner, quieter place to stay between here and the Rio Grande."

Fargo placed an elbow in front of her and lowered his head until he stared directly at her gorgeous mounds. "It has other charms as well, I see. I think I'm going to enjoy my stay."

"I like to give my customers a personal touch you won't find anywhere else," Ellen said softly. "And a few lucky souls get special treatment."

"What does a man have to do to qualify?"

"Be good-looking," Ellen responded, then winked. "Damned good-looking, like you are."

"Lucky me."

"Here," Ellen said, spinning the book toward him. "Jot down your John Hancock and I'll fetch you a key."

Fargo felt her hand lightly brush his when she turned. He admired the saucy swirl to her slim hips as she went through the curtain. His manhood, long denied female company, twitched eagerly.

The ink in the well was nearly dry. Fargo had to poke the pen in a few times before he could finish his signature. Replacing it, he idly gazed through the sparkling front window and noticed Eli and two other men hurrying past, all three staring straight ahead so intently their necks seemed to be locked in place. What was that all about? he wondered. The rustle of smooth fabric on sheer stockings brought him around.

"Here you go, big man." Ellen handed over a key. "Room one twenty-one, the last one on the right. It's nice and peaceful back there. No one will disturb you."

"I'm hoping at least one person will come by," Fargo said, staring her right in the eyes.

A faint pink tinge capped both of Ellen's full cheeks. "You never know. Maybe someone will." She gave a little cough. "I know I have to drop by later. I cleaned your room yesterday and there was no towel over the washbasin."

"I could sure use one," Fargo admitted. "A long time on the trails makes a man whiffy."

"Personally," Ellen said, bending so close their noses nearly touched, "I like your scent just fine. Some men stink to high heaven, like they carry a polecat in their drawers. You sort of remind me of new leather."

"And that's good?"

"I *love* new leather."

Chuckling, Fargo hoisted his bedroll. "There's no rush on the towel," he commented. "I could use a nap before I do anything else."

"Oh?" Ellen sounded disappointed. "All right. I'll wait an hour or so. By then most everyone will be out eating supper. We'll likely have the whole hotel all to ourselves."

"You sure you'd be safe?" Fargo joked.

"Are you sure *you* would?" she countered.

Fargo walked to the hall. He had just entered when a low gasp drew his attention to the counter, where Eleanor Seaver stood gaping at the countertop. "Are you all right?"

"Fine," Ellen said, vigorously bobbing her chin.

"Just dandy. You go get that sleep. I'll be along later like I promised."

The room was close to the rear exit. Fargo had seen plusher accommodations, but few as nicely arranged. He leaned the rifle in a corner, tossed his gear on the chair, and stepped to the sole window. It fronted an alley partially filled with old boxes and empty crates. He raised the sill a few inches to admit fresh air, then lay on his back on the bed, careful not to rake the spread with his spurs.

For the better part of an hour, Fargo tried to doze off. Given his fatigue and the interval since he'd last slept, he figured he would have no problems. But a vague feeling of unease gnawed at the back of his mind, making him toss and turn from one side to the next. He assumed it must have something to do with his current job.

A rich businessman in Waco had offered Fargo a hefty sum to track down the pair of killers responsible for the death of the businessman's son. Ordinarily, Fargo didn't hire himself out as a bounty hunter, but in this case he had made an exception. For two reasons.

First, the man in Waco was a kindly old-timer, his wife of the same mold. Everyone Fargo had talked to in Waco made the same claim. The couple was the kind who would do anything for anyone, and had. They'd reared their son to be the same way. The boy had been their pride and joy, and his murder had left them devastated.

Second, the killing itself had been particularly vicious. Two men had broken into the store and were rifling the safe when they were caught in the act by the son. They'd tied him to a chair, stuffed a gag in his mouth, and pistol-whipped him so badly every bone in his face had been broken. Not satisfied with that, they had kicked and stomped on him until all his ribs were busted, his arms and legs broken, and his internal organs too severely damaged to ever heal. The son had died several days later.

Fargo had been passing through Waco after a short stay in Mexico. Somehow word had gotten to the couple, who had promptly paid him a visit and pleaded for his help. He didn't like to think he was growing soft, but the old woman's tears had touched him deeply. So he'd accepted.

Learning the identities of the two killers had been easy. After pocketing their loot, the pair had brazenly walked out the front door to their horses, mounted, and headed out of town, pausing only once to shoot to ribbons a wanted poster nailed to a pole. It had been a wanted poster of *them*.

Frank and Bob Jeffers were known from one end of Texas to the other as the most cold-blooded bad men ever born. Their string of savage killings went back some ten years, and nothing the Rangers or local law officers had done in all that time had been able to put a crimp in their lawless ways.

In this instance, the marshal of Waco had formed a posse and chased the pair to the limits of his jurisdiction. Later, special Rangers had been sent in, but the trail had grown cold, the clues had dried up. The Jeffers disappeared once again.

Fargo would be the first to admit he had little hope

of finding the vermin. He was a tracker, not a lawman. Give him fresh tracks and he could follow anyone anywhere. But he'd given his word to the Walkers. He'd try his best for two weeks. If he came up empty-handed, he'd send them a wire and head north for Denver.

Now Fargo had only four days to go. He'd followed up lead after lead without result. The latest information, gleaned from a faro dealer in the last town, was that one Jeffers had been seen heading across the Black Prairie. Which explained Fargo's presence in Ripclaw, but not why he couldn't sleep.

Sitting up, Fargo went to the basin and splashed water on his face and neck. Since he couldn't rest, he figured he might as well make himself presentable for when Ellen dropped by. As he turned off the spigot, his keen ears registered a faint scraping noise from out in the hallway.

Guessing it was the brunette, Fargo tiptoed to the door and positioned himself slightly behind it. He'd bid her enter, and when she did, scoop her into his arms. Women liked men who acted on the spur of the moment, who could surprise them, make them laugh. Besides, he wanted to get his hands on those melons of hers.

But Fargo was the one surprised. He had his eyes on the latch and was smirking in anticipation when he heard another noise—the raspy click of a pistol hammer being cocked. Then two more.

Twilight had claimed Ripclaw. In the room it was darker, so Fargo didn't bother hiding. Quickly, he grabbed the wooden chair and planted his feet firmly on the other side of the jamb, where he could see the door opening. Which it did, slowly, a moment later.

Fargo had his broad back flush to the wall. He saw the tip of a revolver barrel poke inside, then a hand, a thick wrist. The outline of a man's face appeared, swinging toward the bed as if the man knew right where it was located. The man took a step, edging inside, and that was when Fargo swung with all his might.

There was a tremendous crash as the chair caught the intruder flush in the face. The chair shattered. The man flew backwards into the corridor, his six-gun blasting once, sending a slug into the ceiling. Someone else cried out and there were two loud thuds.

Fargo slammed the door shut. He dashed to his rifle as the hotel echoed with three gunshots and the top panel in the door was splintered by three bullet holes. Spinning, he spotted a figure beyond the door. Fargo tucked the stock to his shoulders, took a hasty bead, and fired, the roar of the big Sharps near-deafening in the confines of the room.

In the hall someone cursed.

Someone else squawked, "Sweet Jesus! The son of a bitch has a cannon in there!"

"Hush, damn you!" snapped a third man, and a flurry of whispering erupted.

Fargo knew the local law would come running, but he didn't aim to stay there until that happened. Being trapped in the room made him edgy, gave him the same sort of feeling a cornered mountain lion or bear experienced when hemmed in by hunters. He needed room to move, to take the fight to those trying to take his life.

Darting to the window, Fargo eased it as high as it would go. He slipped a boot outside, lowered it to the bare earth. Bending, he eased his shoulders through and was straightening when a hard object jammed into his temple and a gruff voice snarled a warning in his ear.

"Make one more move, you bastard, and your brains will be splattered all over that wall!"

Usually, Fargo made it a practice not to dispute a man holding him at gunpoint. But someone was trying to kick in the door, evidently in the belief he had locked it, and in another few moments the killers would break in and automatically throw lead in his direction. So it was either turn the tables or die, and Fargo had no intention of being planted in an unmarked grave on the Boot Hill of a two-bit town in the middle of nowhere.

The man with the rifle stepped partly into view and shifted his rifle lower. In that split second, Skye Fargo pivoted on his boot heel and speared the muzzle of the Sharps into the man's gut. The man screeched, doubling in torment, his rifle slipping from weakened fingers. Fargo rammed his rifle stock into the man's head and he dropped like a poled ox.

Half the door was gone. Fargo saw several black silhouettes forcing their way inside. He dived as a pistol cracked. The bullet struck the sill, missing him by a fraction. Hitting on his shoulder, Fargo rolled smoothly and shoved erect, palming his Colt as he rose and covering the window.

Suddenly, from the street, a new voice added to the racket. "Here he is! Down the alley! Come on, before he gets away!"

A rifle thundered. Fargo answered once, watched a figure leap around the corner. He whirled and ran, wondering just how many he was up against and where the hell the marshal of Ripclaw had gotten to. Ten feet from the end of the alley, he drew up short. Another figure had appeared, blocking his path. Fargo detected the glint of metal and raised his Colt, taking deliberate aim. His target, though, took one look at him, screamed in terror, flung a rifle aside, and fled.

Not knowing what to make of the man's behavior, Fargo raced around the corner and stopped to reload the Sharps. At the rear of another building fifty feet to the right, a gun cut loose, the shots chipping wood out of the wall behind him. Ducking, he cat-footed to the far side of the hotel.

In the main street men shouted, boots pounded. More yelling came from the alley Fargo had vacated. He shook his head in bewilderment, racking his brain for an explanation as to why a small army of gunmen were after him. So far as he knew, he had no enemies in that part of the country.

Further pondering was cut short by the arrival of another one, a skinny man holding a shotgun. Fargo swung the Sharps as the man lifted his weapon to fire. The stock of the rifle struck the barrel of the shotgun, deflecting it so that the buckshot ripped into the side of the next building. Fargo plowed a fist into the man's jaw and the man crumpled like so much paper.

The gunmen were closing in from all directions.

Fargo sped along the side of the hotel, intending to lose himself in the crowd that was no doubt gathering out front. He was halfway there when several dark figures materialized ahead at the selfsame instant an open window beckoned on his left. Without hesitation, Fargo threw himself inside and landed on soft carpet. Rising into a crouch, he hugged the wall, listening as men ran past. Their footsteps slowed at the rear.

"I thought I saw him!"

"He must have gone back around!"

"Hank, is he over yonder?"

"No sign of him here."

"Look everywhere. He can't get away."

Working swiftly, Fargo closed and latched the window and moved into the dim recesses of the room. Upraised voices seemed to ring the hotel. Shadows flitted across the glass pane, and seconds later a man in a white hat stopped to peer in. Fargo trained his cocked Colt on the gunman's head, but the man moved on.

Relaxing a hair, Fargo stepped to the closed door. He tried the latch, found it unlocked. A considerable commotion had broken out, and a peek into the hallway showed why. Agitated guests milled about in excitement, demanding to know what all the shooting was about. Ellen moved among them, evidently reassuring them all was well.

Fargo shut the door before anyone noticed him. He threw the bolt, then sat in a rocking chair that faced the window. For the time being he was safe. A faint hint of musky perfume hung in the air, and he wondered if the last person to stay here had been a woman.

For the longest time, the hunt went on. Fargo heard them shouting from one end of Ripclaw to the other. He marveled that no one stepped in to quell the disturbance and wished he knew exactly who was after him and why.

It was close to midnight when the uproar quieted. Fargo decided to try for his room. He'd reclaim his belongings, sneak to the livery, and go find a spot in the nearby woods where he could hole up for a while. His hand was closing on the bolt when he heard someone approach the door. Then the latch wriggled, rattling loudly as the person tried to force the door open. Silently, sliding the bolt, Fargo stepped aside.

Light bathed the carpet. The person entered, unsuspecting. Fargo glimpsed cascading dark hair as he pounced, looping his right arm around the woman's throat. "Don't cry out!" he warned. "I won't hurt you if you do as I say."

The woman had tensed and tried to tear free. On hearing his voice, she stopped, standing meekly. "I won't scream, Mr. Fargo, if that's what you're worried about."

Fargo closed the door with a shove of his foot, then walked around in front of Eleanor Seaver. She regarded him as a frightened doe might regard a stalking wolf. "I didn't know who it was," he said. "Sorry if I scared you."

"I'm fine," Ellen said nervously. She played with the frill on her dress a moment. "Pretty clever of you to hide right under their noses. They've been looking everywhere, and here you are in my own room."

"Who are they?" Fargo asked urgently. "Why do they want me so badly?"

"You don't know?"

Fargo shook his head.

"Marshal Lee Howes has deputized twenty men to bring you in dead or alive—preferably slung over a saddle. They say you're a dangerous character, a killer."

"They must have mistook me for someone else," Fargo said. "I'm not wanted anywhere."

"If you say so," Ellen responded skeptically.

"You don't believe me?"

"I'd like to. I truly would. But everyone knows about Kingfish."

Fargo was more confused than ever. Kingfish was the name of the last town he'd stopped at, the place where he'd been told by a faro dealer that one of those he sought had recently passed through. He'd immediately purchased a few supplies, saddled up, and rode out. Nothing else of any consequence had occurred. "What happened there?"

Ellen looked at him in disbelief. "You don't remember killing those people? Were you drunk at the time?"

"What people?" Fargo said, grasping her wrist in annoyance. He was fast losing his patience with the whole business and couldn't wait to get shy of Ripclaw.

"The evening before last a man calling himself Skye Fargo took a room at a small boardinghouse in

Kingfish. Later that night he killed the owners and two boarders and lit a shuck for parts unknown." Ellen paused. "The sheriff sent a wire to our town marshal. Marshal Howes told all the merchants in Ripclaw to be on the lookout for you."

Now Fargo understood the liveryman's reaction on hearing his name, and why Ellen had gasped when she saw his signature. "I'm not the hombre they want," he insisted. "I have to talk to your marshal and set things straight."

"I wouldn't try, if I were you," Ellen said. "He's liable to shoot you on sight."

Just then the door shook to the pounding of a heavy fist, and a deep voice bellowed, "It's the marshal! Open up! I know you're in there."